GOING UNDER

The integrity of a man is evident
from his attitude to the word
LEO TOLSTOY

(LYDIA CHUKOVSKAYA)

Going Under

TRANSLATED FROM THE RUSSIAN
BY
PETER M. WESTON

Quadrangle/The New York Times Book Co.

Asterisks in the text draw the reader's attention to Notes
at the end of the book.

Library of Congress Cataloging in Publication Data

Chukovskaia, Lidiia Koveneevna.
    Going under.

      I. Title.
PZ4.C5593Go5   [PG3476.C485]   891.7′3′42   74-17403
ISBN 0-8129-0510-5

"Here we are! Here is your Litvinovka," said the driver, once again making the wood and the mauve snow turn sharply before my eyes. At the sight of the tiny Finnish houses flying towards me my heart sank. I was hoping to find something different at the end of my journey after three hours in a cold train and an hour in a car. No doubt the wash-basins would be by the entrance, it would smell of the kitchen and damp firewood would be stacked by the stove. The misery of living in winter in a summer house which I so detested. There would be a draught from the windows and from under the doors. . . .

"We've arrived!" Nikolai Aleksandrovich Bilibin, who happened to be travelling with me in the car taking us to the resthome, flung open his winter coat and rummaged at the driver's feet for his brief-case. But the car went on and the pack of the little Finnish houses parted and was left behind; one more turn and the car stopped at the entrance of a large two-storey stone house.

Two young girls in white overalls over their padded coats rushed out into the frost to meet us.

We entered. The girls were carrying our cases.

"Over here, please. Do take off your things", said a stout lady with dyed hair and a beauty spot on her pink face. "Anya, help them with their coats, you can see they're frozen. Take the cases to number 14 and number 8. Are you very cold? Never mind, you'll soon get warm. Make yourselves at home. You can sign the register presently."

After completing the formalities the stout lady, evidently the matron, sailed gracefully ahead of us up a broad staircase of two flights. There were carpets in the guest-room, a shining grand-piano, a gleaming parquet floor. No, this was no *dacha* but rather a comfortable hotel. It was warm and quiet. One could just hear the murmur and tinkling of the central heating. A red carpet stretched the whole length of the corridor. A portentous silence reigned here, unbroken by the sound of footsteps.

The matron opened one door for Bilibin and a little further on another for me.

At last I was at home. From the lounge came the musical deep sound of a clock striking and immediately one could hear the measured assiduous pounding of an electric power-station. At long last I would be living alone in a room, for the first time since the war. It was as though I was in my own home in Leningrad. I would be able to sit down at a desk which would not have to be turned into a dining-table three times a day. I would be able to work in quiet. Thought or imagination would not be knocked down, mutilated by somebody's words from the kitchen . . . I rested the palm of my hand on the blue pipe of the radiator. It was hot.

Within these unfamiliar walls it would at last be possible to recover, to face oneself again.

But it was clear that this meeting with myself was going to be no easy thing because I immediately started trying to avoid it. 'How old could this woman be?' I thought lazily. Her languishing gaze, blond, fashionable hair-do, rings with green square-cut stones on her fingers . . . How she must despise communal flats! It must be very much to her taste to work in such a smart place. 'Writers are such interesting people! But, of course, even writers can sometimes be rude, but on the whole, writing is a free profession and, whatever you say, makes people more refined'. How old could she be? Twenty

6

eight? Thirty eight? She probably misses Moscow and dreams of getting a lift there from time to time to have a manicure and go to the theatre. She must be bored to death by the pure air of this place and by the forest covered in snow.

I took a cautious glance through the window. It was dusk. The wood ran down into a ravine—the snow there was hard-packed—and beyond the ravine little fir-trees had run onto a hillock. They were still young, yellowing like chicks, and on the very top stood the prettiest of them all, slender and youthful. It was the first to reach the top and there it stood. Beyond the little fir-tree lay the village. "Kuzminskoye" the driver had called it. The tiny houses seemed to have been drawn by the clumsy hand of a child. Two crooked lines crossing each other were the roofs, a lopsided, slightly bigger square were the walls and some, smaller, lopsided squares were the doors and the windows.

I switched on the light. Everything vanished—the snow and the little houses.

I drew the curtains and turned round. Now I was face to face with my room. This was where I would be living for twenty-six days. I slowly looked round, apprehensively, carefully. Blue walls, blue pipes, a low, broad bed, a bed-side table, a small rug, a writing desk . . . I promptly put my ink-well and Katya's photograph on the table. I had hoisted my flags! It was here that the meeting would take place; in the presence of this table, these dark curtains and the white muslin curtains in the windows which looked as innocent as the little fir-trees outside.

"Supper is ready," said a young voice in the corridor. And more peremptorily: "Time for supper!"

But I stayed in my room.

I went to bed early last night and slept deeply, without waking until light began to seep through the curtains. I jumped out of bed so as not to be late for breakfast. Indeed, it was already eight o'clock. Having washed and dressed I went down to the dining-room but there was nobody there yet. It was a long room with small, bright windows and round tables. The whiteness of the stiffly starched tablecloths matched the hard crust of the snow in the ravine outside. The tables shone with the china and little pyramids of napkins, but the dining-room was empty. I seemed to be the first. No, sitting at the far table in the corner was a young, slim, dark-eyed woman in trousers who was gracefully breaking an egg with a teaspoon.

A waitress, with an enviable glow on her cheeks, showed me to my place with a friendly smile, carefully noted what I wanted to eat and served me promptly. I gazed through the sparkling clean window: all this was mine! There stood my own fir-tree on the hillock. It looked so touchingly serious. Surely it must have known how lovely it was! The roofs of the houses on the hill, drawn by a child's hand, looked whiter this morning and closer to the ground.

My table was laid for another two people but I didn't wait for my unknown companions. I quickly ate my breakfast and out I went into the fresh air which I hadn't breathed for ages.

I put on my coat and went straight ahead without thinking where I was going. Right by the house the mud was churned up, a little further away there was soft, sickly-looking snow and only in the fields far away in the distance, lay the unrumpled cloth of the frozen snow crust. There was the little house of the director, blue, like a Ukrainian *izba*, a barn, a dog on a chain. Dereliction, dankness, uselessness. I went on. Grey clouds, a grey distant view, a yellow sky showing through the black branches of the trees. How prophetic and terrible it would have been in Leningrad—the yellow sky and the black branches—but here it had no fateful significance, it was merely the yellow light of dawn. I went on, not looking where I was going, past some chickens, past someone's underclothes hanging frozen on a line . . . Ah, that's what it was there! A birch grove!

It was as if there had never been any mud by the house. Here the snow lay rich, thick, just as it was in the ravine by my window. And from the deep snow the birch-trees stretched out to the clouds.

I made my way through the snowdrift and went along a path. All around, everything was grey, crumbly, moisture-laden. The birches grew in families—three, two on a root—straining upwards, and the taller they were the further they leaned apart from one another as though in a motionless but swift waltz. I stopped and threw back my head and at once these evenly swaying tree-tops and slow-moving, grey, swollen storm-clouds made my head go round. The clouds filled the sky so tightly that they seemed to be snowdrifts on another world in the sky. I walked along the path growing tipsy from the flashing, from the circling of the grey and white slender stems, and I was beset by sadness as always happens at moments of a happiness too strongly felt . . . For this would be taken away from me. I would have to give it up. It wasn't that it would be taken away from me just like that, but simply something incomprehensible would pass which we call 'time', the 4th or 9th would turn up in the calendar and at its bidding the car would call at the front door. I would start packing my case and the grove would no longer be mine, access to it would be forbidden to me . . . In the quiet of this warm and comfortable house the throbbing of the power-station on the hill would be heard as before, the chandeliers and the lamps would continue to grow now dim now bright again, the birch-trees would be stretching out from the snow to the clouds lending their crests to the wind . . . And all this would no longer be mine. Finished! No way back! It would be the 4th of the month. Time to leave.

I had only just made the acquaintance of the grove and had already begun to grieve at the inevitable parting with it.

The footpath twisted and doubled back. The birch-trees obediently parted before me, but it was only for appearances sake to lure me on, for in fact they crowded in on me ever more closely and the footpath, to avoid the families growing in clusters, had to resort to guile by doubling back. Up above the wind soughed. Buds like shining beads kept turning over and sparkling in the branches. Buds? In winter? I peered closer. They were droplets of water.

"Taking a walk?"

A large woman, wearing trousers beneath her winter-coat, and carrying under her arm a big handbag bound in metal, was walking towards me. Her powdered face had grown purple from the cold and the skin under her plucked eyebrows was swollen. A dark-skinned blasé-looking man, in a ski-suit, walked nonchalantly behind her. There was something oriental in his beautifully trimmed beard.

"Well, how is Moscow?" he asked me, making a slight

bow. "Still standing, I hope? I'm told you only arrived today. It's such a hellish bore here . . ."

"That's not very polite, Lado" said the woman snapping her bag as though firing a pistol and I guessed that the man standing in front of me was the famous film director, Lado Kancheli—who had recently won a Stalin prize for his film about Stalin's birthplace, Gori.

We were standing on a narrow path huddled close together to avoid stepping into the snow. I felt ashamed of the shabby sleeve of my coat. They asked me how I liked it here, and who was the broad-shouldered man in a thick winter-coat who had arrived with me, and which room they had put me in. But, at last, they walked on.

Prosperous, well-dressed people! I immediately thought of my old coat, my unpermed and untinted greying hair. So I was not going to live here alone with my memories and work, alone with the forest, sky and books, but with other people, the sort of people who were rather bored and needed to be amused. Somehow I hadn't thought about this when I was on my way here —to seclusion. I hadn't envisaged the existence of other people.

I walked on and on and the birch-trees kept spinning round. Any moment now and my own head would start spinning. A dense, visible air hung between the tree-trunks. This grove reminded me in some way of Holland, where I had never been. Everything swollen with moisture, cloudy, heavy, diffuse. At an exhibition of pictures of Ostroumova-Lebedeva* I had seen Holland just like that—heavy, washed out, damp. There are such days in Leningrad too. From the University Embankment it's impossible to make out the gold of St. Isaac's on the other side of the river.

I turned back. I had a place to go to. I would work today without being disturbed by telephone calls, by conversations from the other side of the partition wall, without feeling hurt for Katya's sake who had nowhere to settle down.

I had gone away. Now Katya when she came home from school, could do her homework at the table without disturbing me.

In the distance I could already see the clothes-line with the writhing shirts. And, past the washing, the fir-trees and the light in the entrance of the house.

I stopped to listen. Was anxiety still alive? Yes, it would seem there was no rest from a mother's anxiety. I could, even now, point with my finger to the accompaniment of this friendly, rounded thump to the very spot in the heart, where it lived. Was Katyusha well? Perhaps she had slipped on her way home from school? Perhaps her school-mistress, who insisted that the children should learn by heart the tag: 'one should learn in such a way that it bounces off your teeth', had reduced her to tears? And what of Elizaveta Nikolayevna? But it would be better not to think about Elizaveta Nikolayevna . . .

The lights of the house shone to greet me, a wave of warmth came from the cloak-room. The girl attendant put aside her book and helped me take my things off. The whole of me was soaked through with fresh air— from head to foot. Not just my hat, galoshes, coat but also my cheeks and chest and legs—all of me. The house welcomed me with the reliable warmth of a town house, with its radiators, the brilliance of parquet floors and medical care. I was called to see the doctor. Then came a pine bath. Then they brought me medicine. Both the doctor and the nurse and the fair, snub-nosed girl whom

I found cleaning my room—all of them took a sincere interest in my maladies, the various proceedings, my diet, the hangers in the cupboard for my one and only dress, the colour of the ink I preferred to use . . . Of course, in actual fact they were not really interested in any of this, but it was a good thing that a kindly pretence was a part of their work.

It's not what one usually finds in the world.

You may be waiting in the housing manager's office to make an inquiry. There's no chair, nowhere to sit down. The girl is chatting to her boy-friend. They are discussing whether to go to the cinema today or not. The young fellow has sprawled himself half across the table and is breathing down her nose, flirting with his eyebrows. Fascinated by this game she spoils a form for the fourth time. And there I am still standing.

"Why is there no chair for visitors?"

"You look healthy enough. You can jolly well stand for a while." And handing the young man a photograph she says:

"Whenever you glance at this photo you'll think of the person concerned."

"But I don't wish to stand here and watch you!"

"You can lie down for all I care!"

It was different here.

The girl, wiping the non-existent dust from the desk, enquired whether she should come and tidy up later, whether she was in the way now. She could have been about seventeen years old, some three years older than Katya. She was so slight, fair, frightened—cautiously dusting the ink-well. It was someone else's ink-well, a writer's, and if one broke it there would be no end of a fuss. In any case the orders were: when a guest is writing he is not to be disturbed. With her snub-nosed, round little face, she resembled a cupid, that bronze one which peeped out from behind the lamp on the grand piano in the guest-room. "Am I in the way? I can tidy up later," she said softly.

. . . February 1949

Until now I had managed to be the first in the dining-room and eat on my own but, today, when I came down, after doing the morning instalment of my translation in the quiet of my room, I found two more people sitting at my table.

"You see how well I look after you," said Lyudmila Pavlovna, in exactly the intonation I had imagined she would use when I followed her down the corridor on the day of my arrival.

"I have put you between two interesting men."

Her intonation corresponded so exactly with what I had imagined that I expected her to pronounce the words I had invented about the refining influence of a free profession. But no. She questioned me about what I ate and what I didn't eat.

In the dining-room Lyudmila Pavlovna's buxom person was clad in a white, starched overall. For a moment she sat down at our table on the empty chair and, in the bright light shining through the crystal-clear window, I saw that she was no twenty-eight-year-old and certainly not thirty-eight, but all of fifty and that she desperately wanted to appear slim. Although she was tightly cor-setted she could not conceal her excess of flesh.

The two 'interesting men' were my companions of the car drive, Nikolai Aleksandrovich Bilibin and a young, balding journalist, on the staff of *Literary Gazette*,*

Sergei Dimitriyevich Sablin.

What sort of people were they? It was impossible to say immediately, though they were gay and friendly. In any case, they were undoubtedly worthy of a younger, more elegant woman than I. But they were also very amiable with me, especially Bilibin.

He said:

"After all, Nina Sergeyevna, whether you like it or not, we're twins. We arrived on the same day, came in the same car, and our rooms too, are on the same floor."

There was something about his insistent familiarity and amiability that I didn't quite like. Back in the car I had already shrunk away from it, listening to the deep, beautiful voice of an actor. He was talking all the time to the driver, but I knew that he was talking for my benefit. And for that reason I didn't react.

"On the Ukrainian Front in the spring," he was now recounting to the journalist, "we got completely bogged down in the mud. It was nothing but clay; the cars couldn't get through. What could we do? We envied the peasants—they got around on their oxen very well. Whenever the drivers saw the oxen they would say: "Those are Moo-moo 2's . . . There's a Moo-moo 2!"

The journalist laughed. I didn't. But Bilibin was determined to make me react.

"What are you working on at the moment?" he asked, passing me the cabbage. "Have some. It's got a lot of vitamins in it."

"Well, nothing much . . ." I replied diffidently, "I'm translating."

There was something distinguished and well-groomed in his slow, lazy movements, in his broad shoulders. He had the big hands of a working man, but his nails were well cared for and long.

15

The men waited patiently for me to finish my sweet. From the next table came the sound of a handbag snapping shut, corks popping and laughter. It was the film director, who, despite the early hour, was treating his lady-friend to some wine. The large white collar on her dress and her luxuriant golden curls were much fresher than her face.

"Not many people in the dining-room today," she said, casting a glance round the room. "I suppose not all the guests who're living here have come down yet."

". . . living here? Who's living with whom?" the film director asked with a bored expression.

Bilibin was telling me and the journalist about his new novel. I hadn't even read the old ones. The novel was about coal-miners in Siberia, advanced technical methods of mining ore, the introduction of mechanization. The conflict over production was closely interwoven with family differences. The novel had already been practically accepted by *Znamya*—he had only been asked to expand slightly the role of the Party organizer.

"And here I am spending six hours a day expanding the Party organizer," said Bilibin, turning towards me his large face with its high forehead and thin nose, and looking squarely at me with his tranquil, yellow eyes. "That's why I came here."

There was no mockery in his eyes, but although they were wide open and looking directly at me, I had the impression that they were veiled by something.

I got up from the table. My companions accompanied me to the door.

"You're already looking much better," said Bilibin to the slim, dark-eyed woman who was coming towards us. She smiled, revealing small, even teeth. "Don't be afraid, don't be afraid; I don't bring bad luck! I haven't got an evil eye!"

I went up to my room.

During the night I woke up with my heart thumping. Tears were flowing down my hair and tickling my ear.

Something terrible had happened, but what it was I couldn't remember. I couldn't recall the dream itself, only the horror I experienced.

I lay on my wide, soft bed. Blood pounded in my ears, my heart couldn't quieten down after the shock.

All around lay the quiet of the night. Solid, black. I wanted to touch it with my hand, feel its consistency like feeling material.

One couldn't turn on the light as the power-station didn't function at night. In any case, with this terror in the heart it was easier to exist like that, without light.

What was it? I could feel my heart beating in my throat, ears, temples. It filled my chest with a hot pounding and, it seemed to me, the room also. I must have dreamt of Alyosha's death again.

But which one? What kind of death? In transit? In camp? Under interrogation?

I knew nothing of his end and so any end was fit for my imagination.

But ever since that conversation on the stone steps near the water, that conversation in the autumn, the dream of Alyosha's death under interrogation kept coming back to me. How many times had I already dreamt of his death? It would be possible to count up the exact number from the diary, but then I never had my diary with me . . . But I could reckon it up without it.

17

It began in the autumn of 1940 in the fine rain, when a girl-friend of mine suddenly made a date with me on the embankment and we went down the steps to the black water with its icy breath. There, down below, by the water, on those flat granite slabs, there it was safe. There was no one, nothing. There she told me about an interrogation of which she had heard from her cousin, who in turn, had been told under oath by a man, released in 1939. Until then, of course, we had had a pretty good idea, but didn't dare to believe it. Now our conjectures had proved true and we learnt for certain why everybody always confessed and slandered one another. I had asked her on that occasion about the finger. 'What do you think, how many minutes could you stand having your finger crushed in a door?' And she had said in reply: 'What about you?'

And ever since that time—it would soon be ten years—this dream had come to haunt my nights, a dream of the interrogation and Alyosha's death under interrogation.

But tonight it was different. I peered into the pitch darkness of the room, as though the outlines of the vanished dream could still be preserved in it.

Tonight I dreamt of some different death of Alyosha. Which one then? In the railway carriage? No, it was not that.

And why did I always dream of his death under interrogation? No doubt dreams are like that. If you dream a dream once, you can expect it again and again. But why did the end come always whilst under interrogation? Alyosha, after all, had also been taken somewhere, had been sent somewhere. How the dates were engraved on my memory! At the prison window on the 5th of January they told me: 'He's left'. Where to? 'He'll write to you himself'. Two days later, in the Office of the Public

Prosecutor they said: 'Ten years without right of correspondence, with confiscation . . . When he's released he'll send you a letter.' It meant that after all the interrogations there was still something further to come, but I kept on dreaming of nothing but interrogations. It was probably because it was impossible to dream of the unknown; the transit of prisoners, the concentration camp. And until now I had never met anyone who had come from there—from a concentration camp. For me this was a horror without colour or smell. But this is no impediment for a dream. In fairy-tales dreams always talk. That is what makes them dreams. Dreams have their own peculiar ways. They come when they want and show us what they want. Take, for example, that same dream 'Alyosha's death under interrogation'. Although I had been told what an interrogation was like, in actual fact I dreamt of it in quite a different way. It should have been like this: a table, paper an interrogator, a chair, a lamp, night and two thugs coming in to beat you up. But each time I dreamt of heavy, black water, exuding cold. Water and silence. Yes, I could see the silence. It swirled up like steam. Swirls of silence. And that was Alyosha under interrogation. People were shoving him with sticks towards the water. Also in silence. He got nearer and nearer to the edge of the granite steps. One of his feet had already lost its grip—the other foot would do so at any moment . . . And that was 'Alyosha's death under interrogation'. I would cry out and wake up. My heart would be banging away like the wheels of railway carriages over rail joints.

But tonight Alyosha's end had been somehow different. A different kind of horror.

I turned over onto my back and now tears flowed down into both my ears.

19

What an impenetrable darkness! It was this darkness which had swallowed up in its maw my vanished dream.

But suddenly it thrust itself out of the darkness.

I remembered what had woken me up. The dream was still there, quite near. It had not yet left the room and that was probably why I managed to seize it.

It was not the death of Alyosha, it was his return. Horror at his return. He had returned, but not to me.

I had already had this dream twice.

Alyosha, it turned out, was alive. I learned of this from a third party, from a friend of Alyosha. I didn't know him, I only knew that he was Alyosha's friend. We were in Katya's nursery. The parquet floor was gleaming like a pinkish-yellow spot and I was thinking in my dream that Elvi, the nanny, had polished the floor today for a special occasion. Alyosha's friend didn't look me in the face, but somewhere to one side, and I understood from this look that Alyosha was alive, that his friends knew where he was but that he didn't want to see me. I was guilty. Alyosha had passed judgement on me, condemned me to perpetual separation. But for what?

> 'Did I not do my best?
> Did I not give him all?
> Such was my love for him
> That I was afraid to tell'.*

I was lying on a low soft bed. A fathomless black silence. My heart was beating as if I had been performing under the big top of a circus, had lost my hold and fallen into the safety net. Tonight I understood where my guilt lay. I understood it from my dream. I was alive. This was it. I was living, going on living after they had shoved Alyosha into the water with sticks. He had come back for a moment to reproach me. That was what my dream was about.

In the guest-room they were playing cards and chess, flirting, reading newspapers and listening to the radio.

'Contract' could be heard from the corridor above the insistent voice of the radio announcer, 'One down'. 'Chicane', 'Pass all round'. 'Another game?'

I went into the guest-room. After all, one should read newspapers!

Bilibin at once broke off his game of cards and drew up a large armchair for me. I took up *Pravda*. Bilibin, the film director, the dark-eyed lady and the journalist were playing Preference. The director's girl-friend was sitting a little way off in a low armchair, pretending to listen to the radio. 'Each new volume of the works of Comrade Stalin makes an inestimable contribution to the idealogical wealth of mankind'—the speaker was saying.

It seemed to me there was something touching and innocent in the slender neck of the dark-eyed woman and in the thin gold chain and stone pendant, which disappeared into the low neck of her dress. She was so pretty, gay, smart. She couldn't have been a writer. She was probably someone's wife.

As always, nothing came of my reading the papers. It was a strange business. I did my best to read them. I could read, but learn something from them—no. The letters formed words, words lines, lines paragraphs, paragraphs articles, but nothing formed thought, feelings or images.

'The Soviet government and the victory of the collective farm system have saved the collective farmers from the catastrophe of drought. The Party and government have given nationwide significance to the urgent struggle against the drought. The great plan for the transformation of nature is a new manifestation of the Bolshevik Party's and the Soviet government's paternal solicitude for our country.'

I read, but saw only the print or some kind of shorthand symbols. 'Nationwide significance'—two words which very conveniently coalesced into one. They could be expressed by one single symbol. 'The great plan for the transformation of nature'—these eight words could also be expressed by one symbol. How many years was it since I had worked as a shorthand typist yet I would still trace automatically in my mind or on my knee the symbols of standard expressions and phrases . . . As I hadn't learned anything about the struggle against the drought I thought I'd better try to read about chess. 'As an essential element of socialist culture chess has become the means of the cultural education of the peasant masses.'

I tried to visualize boys and old men sitting at chessboards in their *izbas* but I didn't succeed. My hand mechanically formed the symbols for 'essential element' and 'the means of the cultural education of the masses'. Symbols. Terms. Behind them were neither *izbas* nor snow-drifts . . . I put the paper to one side.

Could it be that the reason why I had never been able to learn anything from the papers was that in actual fact I wanted to learn about one thing only? It was just about this one thing that the papers never wrote.

"I still think it's better in the sanatorium in spring," said the dark-eyed woman taking her cards from Bilibin (he was dealing), "whatever you may say, it's more fun when it's warm. Each spring I feel irrepressible emotions awakening in me, just as in nature . . ."

Her neck no longer seemed touching to me. An ordinary white neck. On the other hand the film director grew very lively.

"Is that so?" he asked with interest. "What exactly do you feel each spring?"

The woman sitting by the radio turned a knob and the radio wailed stridently like a siren. "Heavens!" shouted Ladu, "you should leave it alone if you don't know how to do it!"

I opened the *Literary Gazette*. Bilibin was gathering up the cards. Evidently they had finished playing. 'Soviet Literature on the up and up' ran the headline in the first column.

After the list of 'works loved by the people' which 'exert a vast influence' I read a paragraph on Pasternak, who 'shunning the great achievements of the people, preferred to rummage about in his own soul'.

"Now, you see, apart from playing cards there's nothing else to do," said the dark-eyed woman, capriciously. "But in the spring it's so beautiful."

"You rarely visit the guest-room," Bilibin said to me, ingratiatingly, after thanking his partners and drawing his chair closer to me.

"You always try to slip past us sinners into your room as quickly as you can. You are a recluse."

The yellow eyes looked at me sharply, observantly, as if calling out to me with their glance. But the next instant they seemed to close again.

I explained that I was working on a very demanding translation, and in any case the doctor had ordered more exercise and also the various treatments took up time. There was simply no time to sit in the guest-room.

"But even when you go out for a walk you seem to

want to be alone," said Bilibin. "If you're really not trying to avoid us, let's take our dear old Sergei Dimitriyevich and go out together for a walk after supper. All right?"

There was nothing I could do. So after supper all our table—Bilibin, the journalist and I, set out. Ah! So the showy walking-stick with its knob shaped like a wolf's head and the luxurious winter coat with its otter fur-collar, were the journalist's. Many times, putting on my own things, I had wondered whose they could be. So that's the sort of person he was!

We strode along the broad, asphalted road because it was the only place lit by lamps. It was cold. We were descending towards the stream, arm in arm. It was quiet, snowy and peaceful as it can only be in the countryside. Only the ticking of the power-station seemed out of place and reminded one of town. But I soon ceased to hear it. The dark forest along the road, the ravine below, the shining stars above were clad in silence. We walked in step down the slope of the hill, trying not to slip. We descended still lower, closer to the stream, I enjoyed striding in step with them, hiding my frozen hands under their sleeves and listening to their slow, quiet talk. "You haven't forgotten your matches?" "They say a lot of people are coming tomorrow, so Lyudmila Pavlovna told me." "They're going to try out a new cook." "Hm . . . I hope they'll try a new sweet rather than a new cook." The silence of the snow, the trees, the sky was so overwhelming that at first we, too, wanted to keep silent, or, if to speak, then only a little and softly. "Your feet aren't frozen are they?"

The trees approached the road in a tall, dark, uneven formation. A solid wall of fir-trees and above them a brilliant moon.

"Look, a grave" said the journalist and jumped with ease over a ditch, nearer the forest.

Bilibin and I stopped.

Sergei Dimitriyevich bent down and touched the white, low, oval hillock, with its neat covering of snow, as though stroking its back.

"Big battles were fought here," said Bilibin. "The winter of '41 . . . There's a poet, wearing his medals, who occupies a table by the window. The third table . . . He's a Jew. Have you seen him? He is a thick-set man, going grey. His name is Veksler. He fought here, they were driving the Germans out of Bykovo."

We stood still for a while. The little mound covered with snow showed white in front of us. The journalist jumped back across the ditch onto the road and again took my arm. We walked on in semi-darkness, to which our eyes were now accustomed.

A bridge rang beneath our feet. The snow lay evenly and neatly on the railings in a long, stick strip. "Listen, you can hear the stream, it's not frozen," said the journalist.

We stopped. I freed my hands from under their sleeves. We went up, each one separately, to the railing.

"No, you can't hear it," said Bilibin.

"Yes, you can. Listen," insisted the journalist.

I stopped to listen. It was a pity to spoil the cloth of snow but the journalist, in any case, had already put his stick on the railing and so I didn't mind disturbing the snow with my elbow. When, for some reason, the journalist took off his spectacles, I saw that his face was kind and child-like, as though the foppish coat and stick were not his at all.

"Yes, I can hear it," I said.

"You're quite right, sometimes it comes, sometimes it

disappears," admitted Bilibin. "Let's stay here for a while."

We stood looking at the forest and at one another, listening to the thump of the power-station and the childish babble of the stream audible above it.

"What's new in the paper today?" asked Sergei Dimitriyevich. "I believe you've read it? I haven't even looked at it. How a period of rest demoralizes one! I don't even read my own paper. For ten days now I haven't opened it, and that's the truth."

"Nothing in particular," I replied.

It occurred to me that rest had probably nothing to do with it. The presence of the forest, the snow, the little fir-tree on the hill—that's what forbids one to read the papers.

'At the sound of music' came into my mind.

"Apparently Pasternak has again been censured," said Bilibin, as if in reply to my thought. From the noncommittal way he said it, it was impossible to gather whether he approved of the censure of the poet, or not.

"Who wrote the piece?" asked the journalist.

"I can't remember the name. He quotes some verses and says they're incomprehensible."

"He does, in fact, write somewhat incomprehensibly," said the journalist, in a faintly reproachful tone. "My wife read aloud to me some of his poetry recently and it even made us laugh. We couldn't understand anything. It doesn't read very easily. And if we ourselves can't understand it then how can one expect ordinary people to understand?" He paused reproachfully. "Of course, there's no arguing, Pasternak is very talented, both the alliteration and the form are beautiful and so on, but he doesn't think of the sense. It's too obscure. Try to read it to the girls here—Anya, Liza—from Bykovo or Kuzminskoye, they wouldn't understand a word."

"Yes, of course," Bilibin agreed quickly.

I didn't speak immediately. I had to get my breath back. Now I detested the kind, short-sighted eyes of the journalist and the cautious voice of Bilibin and the fact that we had just been silent together.

"And do you think they could understand Baratynsky?"* I said, trying to speak slowly and quietly. "The girls from Bykovo? And what about Fet?* I doubt it. For poetry to them is a completely unaccustomed way of thinking. So you want to throw out our classics as well, do you? Give them away to the Germans? Just because Anya and Liza who only learned to read yesterday, can't understand them . . . and who've been brought up on Dolmatovsky* . . . And what about you? Do you understand the so-called classics? Pushkin for example? I doubt it. You've simply grown accustomed to thinking from your school-days that he's comprehensible . . ." I didn't glance at my companions but looked somewhere into space. "And why do we imagine that we are always capable of understanding the poet in everything? After all, he's ahead of us. He's created by this forest, this language, this people and sent on far in advance, so far that he disappears from the view of those who sent him. And our task, the task of those who know how to read, is to try with all our power to understand him, and having understood, to bring it home to Anya, to Liza. But we shirk our duty and betray . . . both the poet and Anya . . . who, if she understood would rise above herself . . . And if not Anya, then her children. We proudly say we don't understand, but what is there to be proud of in actual fact? Puskin wrote: 'We must be at one with a genius'."

I turned and went up the hill alone. All this had long

been seething inside me, ready to come out, and had suddenly come pouring out at the journalist's words 'my wife and I were reading in the evening and it made us laugh'. There was so much self-satisfaction in that 'my wife and I'! A connoisseur of poetry, indeed! A member of the staff of *Literary Gazette*! I found it difficult to breathe from rage and the climb up the hill. I stopped, so that my companions could catch me up and to get my breath back. I could see their large, dark figures slowly coming towards me from the bridge as though moving in dark water. Alone, without me, they had probably shrugged their shoulders and smiled at each other. A minute ago it would have seemed to me shameful, treacherous cowardice to hold my peace, but now I already felt ashamed of my intemperate words. Who was I talking to! They had nothing whatsoever to do with me! What on earth possessed me to be so frank!

"We must apologize to you, Nina Sergeyevna," Bilibin said briskly, taking my arm. "It was not nice. Indeed, it was impolite on our part to talk like that about your favourite poet. But all the same, you should make some allowance for us. After all, we didn't know that you're so fond of him. And I must admit that there was a good deal of truth in what you said."

I wanted to get back to the house as quickly as possible, home to the quiet of my blue room. The lights of the house, bright as in a town, were shining to welcome us. Now the warmth of their sleeves made me feel uncomfortable. Why had I humiliated myself by my bluntness in front of strangers? I wanted to be alone. I was walking fast and they were compelled to quicken their pace to keep up with me.

Today was a happy day.

I slept soundly, jumped out of bed in the morning and, still bare-footed, parted the curtains. Outside the window everything was sparkling. The little fir-tree, which had run up onto the hill, was no longer green, but white. The brilliant winter had begun!

Trying not to despise myself for my stupidity of the previous day, I quickly dressed and went down to breakfast. Both my companions, clean-shaven and cheerful-looking, were already sitting at the table. Today they treated me as though I were a loaded gun, making sure not to touch off the trigger. I felt amused. They had been landed with an awkward companion. I tried as hard as I could to be dull, and did not once talk about anything beyond Lyudmila Pavlovna's hair-do, the weather and the menu. They passed me the cream, expatiated on its health-giving qualities, retrieved the pepper from another table, and in each studiously polite gesture I felt their fright at what had happened the previous day. No, not at the truth of what I had said, but simply at over-impetuous, excitable conversations which, to say the least, were out of place in a rest-home. After all, everyone had come here to rest, so why argue? We should breathe fresh air and take vitamins! We lived enough on our nerves in town as it was!

Immediately after breakfast, when Bilibin and Sergei Dimitriyevich had sunk down into soft arm-chairs in the guest-room—to smoke—I rushed off to the hall to put on my things. Bilibin followed me with his glance but did not get up.

I dressed quickly lest I should be followed. I wanted to get out there into the sparkling whiteness as quickly as possible—and alone. I could already hear their voices in the hall as I let go the heavy front door behind me. The icy air burned my forehead, and when I took a breath I felt as though I had swallowed a sharp piece of ice. I wanted to stand for a moment by the entrance to take in a glance the icy brilliance which had been given to me with such surprising simplicity and generosity, but the voices behind were catching me up and I almost ran across the little square in front of the house, past the director's home, past the frozen washing, away into the grove. I found myself on the footpath between tall, frothy snow-drifts and, at length, stopped to look round. The fragile word 'sparkling' puckered my lips. How exactly it fitted this ice-covered pattern of branches! Sparkling! The word was brittle like a thin, sharp twig, like tiny, green and blue sparks, playing in the snow at the foot of the birch-trees. The very word made my teeth go cold.

I walked slowly along the path, took off a glove and lightly touched the snow of a drift. It felt hard today. Its stiff, sparkling crust stung. Birch-trees stood close by, as though sculpted out of white silence. The tree-tops disappeared into the sky. It seemed to me that the fragile, white branches must ring out as they touched the vault of heaven. I was sure that, up there, there was a gentle tremulous ringing.

The scrape of footsteps startled me. Could it be my friends? No. Along the footpath a young girl in a shawl, padded coat and felt boots was walking towards me. The shawl made her face look round. The apples of her cheeks were red.

"Hello!" she said in a clear voice and stepped into deep snow leaving the path to me. If the birch-tree itself, I thought, had wanted to say hello to me, it would have given me its greeting in just such a frosty, clear voice.

The grove soon ended. Far away, on the crest of the

hill, the village of Bykovo had buried itself in the snow. In front of the village, fields stretched out like a snowy plain and beyond stood the forest. Sledge tracks, smoothed down and gleaming, ran over a field towards the village.

> . . . Let us visit the empty fields,
> The forests recently so thick,
> The shore which was so dear to me,*

suddenly came to my mind and it became clear to me that I had understood these verses for the first time. So this is what they were about! And that shore was the shore of happiness. The last line brought tears to my eyes and the tears, like everything today, like the air I breathed, were stinging.

> ". . . so dear to me!—"

This he wrote about happiness, perhaps about present happiness, perhaps about happiness already lost, past . . .

> "Skimming over the morning snow,
> Dear friend, let us feel the stride
> Of the impatient steed.
> Let us visit the empty fields,
> The forests recently so thick,
> The shore which was so dear to me."*

These "ski's", and "sn's" and "st's" were the slippery brilliance of the sleigh-path, crossing the field. The flashing of the sleigh-runners. And the "dear shore" was a memory of happiness.

Perhaps the shore was dear to him for the very reason that they would soon see it together?

I took the sledge track, screwing up my eyes against the glare of mica. And suddenly it occurred to me that the Germans had been here. They had walked here, along this road, from this village to the grove, eight years ago. I knew that before, but the thought astonished me as if I had just learned it for the first time.

'And let us visit the empty fields'—they could not understand this line. What right then had they to walk about here, leaving their tracks in the snow? For them this was not a field or a forest, but territory, a place.

'Let us visit' one says usually if going to see friends, but Pushkin said it of the field and forest. The trees and river were for him like beloved friends.

All at once I felt very tired. It must have been the intense white glare. I turned back and losing my way from time to time in the snow trudged slowly home. I watched only the ground and no longer saw the birch-trees or the drifts of snow. The sparkling silence was so abundant, I felt it was too much for me to bear.

> The kingdom of whiteness and silence
> Instils in my heart a fear.
> I whisper: "I thank you!" quite softly.
> 'You're giving me more than I ask.'*

. . . February 1949

By now I knew when quiet descended on this house. It was when neither the clatter of dominoes in the guest-room, nor the smooth footsteps of Lyudmila Pavlovna, nor the obtrusive voice of the radio could be heard. There was only the kindly, indefatigable ticking of the power-station. It happened three times a week, of an evening, when our "cultural officer"* came over with a new film. Everybody would go off to watch it. At these times I could risk going under, freed from the fear that by some sound or word—as used to happen in town—you would be dragged back to the surface. The telephone would ring. Who could it be for? A bell would ring in the hall—was it four times? The sound of wrangling came from the kitchen right next to my door. Elizaveta Nikolayevna was nagging Aunt Dusya again. It was as though one was being dragged up the stairs by the feet, with one's forehead banging against each step. The deeper I managed to go under the more painful and lengthy was the process of being dragged out.

"What sort of pearl-barley soup do you like?" Aunt Dusya was asking. "Thickish or thin?"

"Soup should be as it should be," Elizaveta Nikolayevna answered and her pomposity set my heart pounding. A crude and ruthless nature, never ashamed of itself, was evident in her every word, in every step. She was ashamed neither of cruelty nor of vulgarity. She had once uttered the sentiment: "Borshch is characterized by beet-root."

I would always remember when I once had a very bad migraine and Katenka asked Aunt Dusya not to make a noise in the kitchen. Elizaveta Nikolayevna asked Dusya for something or other and she answered in a whisper.

"What are you whispering for all the time?" shouted Elizaveta Nikolayevna. "Talk like a human being."

Aunt Dusya explained to her: "Nina Sergeyevna is sick."

"There are no sick people in my house," Elizaveta Nikolayevna replied haughtily, without lowering her voice. She went along the corridor to her room, clacking her heels.

I would never forget how, during the war, another neighbour of ours, an unfortunate woman with a large family, whose husband had been killed, began selling off her wretched bits and pieces. She bothered Elizaveta Nikolayevna with some nightdresses.

"I don't wear such nightdresses," replied Elizaveta

Nikolayevna. The nightdresses were neither foreign nor for export, but very ordinary.

It seemed to me that only at that point in time did I begin to understand the reason for her pride. All her life she had been an unremarkable married woman, then an unremarkable widow. All her life she had had two occupations: visiting second-hand shops and persecuting her daily help. Where did her self-assuredness come from? Why did she always behave as though she had performed some enormous service? She almost seemed to be Galina Ulanova* and Anna Akhmatova* rolled into one. And it was not the class or caste arrogance of the academic but a profound conviction of the greatness of her own person. "I don't wear such night-dresses."

She had never had any children; she didn't know how to be a good housewife, sew, mend, bake pies, buy berries in season and sugar for jam. Being a good housewife, to her way of thinking, meant finding fault with, persecuting and putting the servant in the wrong.

"What on earth have you brought?" she shouted at Aunt Dusya in the kitchen. "It's stinking. Smell it. Go on, take a deeper breath! Hold it closer to your nose, it won't bit you! I thought I was sending an experienced cook to the market and here like some stupid girl you bring me a stinking goose . . ."

"But I am not a cook, Elizaveta Nikolayevna, I told you so in advance. I can only help around the house. I have no place of my own, as you know. I lost it in the war. Otherwise, do you think I'd go out to work for people . . . And it isn't stinking . . ."

"You're not a cook? Pray, what are you? A professor's wife? I don't know. I took you on as a cook . . . Go back to the market, sell the goose and bring me the money.

34

And don't start howling. I am not your Victor Petrovich . . ."

Victor Petrovich! It was five years since his death and the memory of his kindness and gentleness with people was still troubling the inconsolable widow.

He was completely under her thumb. Even Katya would show surprise and whisper to me: "I would beat her!" Sometimes our poor Victor Petrovich would rebel, but would soon give in and repent. And we would hear her distinct voice saying, shamelessly unconcerned with her neighbours:

"Stop whining! Rather than make a scene you should have your liver seen to!" And Elizaveta Nikolayevna would go off to the hairdresser's, having given strict orders to Dusya not to run around in her absence after Victor Petrovich with drops and poultices, but to get on with the business and prepare the accounts for the week. Now, when she was no longer near, I recalled her straight back and the proud tilt of her head, and understood at long last that it was just this constant, inevitable, complete domination over one human soul that gave her such a high opinion of herself. One person, just one person, had submitted to her unconditionally, completely and utterly. And this was enough for the assertion of her ego.

How many descents she had spoiled for me! That's why I had remembered her today, when for the first time since my arrival I had tried to go under. Even here, with more than a hundred kilometres separating us, the thought of her violence and rudeness and the certainty that there, in the town, Katyusha, doing her lessons, would hear that hard voice from the other side of the partition-wall, prevented me from making the descent.

Nevertheless the first descent did take place today. It was still only experimental, of short duration. I was only testing it and trying to persuade myself not to be afraid. I could still see my room. I kept glancing at my watch. I jumped when the door banged downstairs. The impenetrable mass of water, protecting my soul from encroachment, had not yet closed above my head and had not yet formed a barrier between me and the world.

But now I believed it would close.

. . . Was it not strange that this diving to the bottom in company with Leningrad, Katenka, the Neva by night, that this secret sound, audible only to me, which sprang from the intermingling of silence and memory, should later on acquire flesh? Should with the aid of ink, paper and print obtain the commonplace, universally accepted name, accessible to all, of book?

"Have you read 'Going Under' yet?"

"No. What's it about? Divers?"

"Don't bother to read it. It's very boring."

"No, it's not. You must read it! The book has got something. If you like I'll bring it? There's nothing about divers."

The book . . . It would stand on the shelves with other books, it would be picked up, the pages turned over, then put back again. The dust would be wiped off, dust of the quiet of this place, of today, through which Alyosha's voice and little Katya's tears came back to me.

The book was me, the sinking of my heart, my memories, which nobody could see, just as nobody could see, for instance, a migraine, a point of pain in my eye, but it would become paper, binding, a new book on the market and—if I were to plumb the depths fearlessly—someone's new soul. In creating it, Alyosha's voice and Katya's tears would permeate this soul.

"It's the same as a grove," the thought occurred to me today. "Yes, a birch-grove with its tree-tops rustling in the sky. It becomes first firewood, then burns in a stove—and then—then gives warmth to someone, who gazes into the hot flames."

However, all that was nonsense. No-one would gaze into my fire. Why, then, bother to go under? For even if my spoils were turned into a manuscript—into paper and ink—they would never be turned into a book. In any event not before my death.

Why then did I descend? To get away from myself?

No, for the place where I went away to was even more frightening than being here on the surface. There I could hear the heavy footsteps of the soldiers taking Alyosha away, there was our staircase, down which he went stepping lightly and quickly between the soldiers and turning round as he went and smiling so that I should not be afraid. There was our felt-lined door. For some reason I had carefully fastened all the locks and bolts after them as soon as their footsteps had died away. (What was the sense of fastening them if he had already been taken away?) . . . There was little Katya who didn't wake up when he took her up from her bed and hugged her for the last time. There were noiseless cars one after the other, one after the other, extinguishing their lights at the prison gates.

There lay the question which had haunted me for so many years. What was his last moment like? How had they turned a living man into a dead man? I no longer asked for what? I only asked, "How?" "Where?" "When?" And where had I been a that moment? Had I been with him? Had I been thinking about him?

And where was his grave? What was the last thing he had seen as life abandoned him?

There he was walking down out staircase, surrounded by soldiers, turning round and smiling to me not to be afraid. What happened then? The prison gates, I knew them well. I had stood before them. And then—the interrogation. That I also knew. Both in reality and in my dreams. And afterwards?

No, no-one would permit my memories to be turned into a book. Nor the question which had been gnawing at me.

Why, then, did I make my descent?

I wanted to find brothers—if not now, then in the future. All living things seek brotherhood and I sought mine. I had been writing a book to find brothers, even if only there in the unknown distance.

. . . *February 1949*

Today was an alarming day, perhaps also joyful, but nevertheless alarming. It was as though I was again in the world, and not here, protected by the small, green fir-tree, in this unreal life.

Over tea the journalist told us some literary news (he had just been phoning Moscow, in a loud voice and at length.) Big changes were expected in the Union of Writers.* The leaders had not been sufficiently tough in their fight against cosmopolitanism. Semskoy was to be the secretary in place of Belenky. A change of editors was expected on the paper *Soviet Writer.*** Bilibin's face darkened for an instant, his eyes gleamed with zeal, unfeigned interest.

"Do you know if Tukmanov will be staying on?" he asked quickly. (Tukmanov was his editor.)

"I think so," answered Sergei Dimitriyevich. "Anyhow, nobody said anything against him . . . And how's your book progressing?"

"Well, every morning I work from around seven . . . I'm doing what the editors wanted . . . Here and there I have to prune it, here and there develop. So I go on tapping away without stopping . . . The noise of the typewriter doesn't disturb you, Nina Sergeyevna?"

He just had to evoke some sort of response from me, every time.

"No, not in the least."

What a strange face he had. Every time he turned his head he looked different. In profile, his head had something sharp, hawk-like about it. In fact there was something rather common and even slightly womanish in his features. I noticed today that he had two deep pockmarks, one on his chin, the other on his cheek. Every day I discovered something new. His brows were short and slanting. They looked like stress marks over his eyes, made his gaze sharp and hawk-like.

I got up and went to put on my things. It was time for my walk—before going under. I had already done the obligatory daily instalment of my translation that morning and was preparing to undertake a descent after tea, when they had all gone off to the cinema. If I succeeded in bringing the sky, snow and air to my writing-desk it would be easy to go under and that happy clarity of vision would come more quickly. But Bilibin got up at the same time as I and followed me with such unhurried naturalness that to all intents and purposes we might have agreed beforehand to go for a walk together. In the hall he politely helped me on with my coat. "Developing the party organizer," I thought, maliciously, looking once more into his tranquil, yellow eyes. "You'll manage it . . . you clown!"

"I won't be in the way if I come with you? My doctor was very emphatic that I should take a walk after tea, before supper."

"No, not in the least," I replied once more. We set off. It was dark, cold, slippery. The cold seemed damp. There were no stars, no moon. Bilibin took my arm. We walked along the path to the road in silence. I felt annoyed that he didn't speak, and still more that his silence alarmed me.

"To tell the truth, Nina Sergeyevna, I still can't forgive myself," Bilibin began in his beautiful voice. We had reached the street lights, turned off to the right and began to descend towards the bridge.

"For what?" I asked, freeing my arm.

"For that conversation we had here on this very spot. How furious you were with me and Sergei Dimitriyevich. Afterwards I was so annoyed that our tastes in poetry are so different that I really wanted to throw myself off the bridge into the river. I really did! Do you really like that Pasternak so much?"

His voice had a sincere and heartfelt ring about it. Yet in the tone of his voice, not even the tone but rather the undertone, there was something veiled.

"It isn't a question of me being very fond of him," I said patiently. "It's not him I'm sorry for, but you. How lightly you forego our great pleasures at someone else's instigation . . ."

"But, as they say, there's no accounting for taste. One can't argue about taste . . ."

I had expected this sort of empty answer, and I didn't start to argue, although when one came to think about it, what were people to argue about if not taste? Did not love for a poet or hatred or indifference spring from the depths of the soul? Could it possibly be a chance phenomenon? Was there not here a watershed, a frontier? Surely there was no better way to determine friendship or enmity, distance or nearness than by what poems and what lines in those poems one loved?

"I tell you what," Bilibin said, suddenly, "let's turn off here onto this path into the forest. Look, the moon's come up. It's large, a full moon. Don't be afraid, it won't be dark."

We turned off. He took my arm again, firmly, securely. The path was narrow and we had to walk close together. The pale blue and yellow moon had settled down comfortably on the branch of a fir-tree, as though it had been there for centuries. Little pools of light danced on the steep snow-drifts. "What a banal situation! A moonlight walk in the forest," I thought, "with an attractive man. It would just suit Ludmila Pavlovna . . . What will he talk about next? We've already talked about poetry. It's time to go on to love. On an abstract, philosophical plane of course . . . for the first time."

Indeed, he started to talk, but not about love at all. The walk did not develop along the usual lines of a sanatorium flirtation.

"Look how the forest has been ruined here," he said. "You, as a city dweller, walk along, thinking that before you lies a dense and magnificent forest. But, in fact, the trees are eaten up."

He suddenly left me, jumped across a ditch and with snow up to his ankles stopped under a tall fir-tree. He looked young in the moonlight with his coat unbuttoned on his chest. His face, bathed in the moon, had lost its wrinkles; the pockmarks had disappeared from his chin and cheek. His face seemed youthful, full of spirituality . . . Once again a different face.

Carefully parting the branches so as not to scatter

snow on himself he went up to the tree-trunk. Then he took some moss from the bark and rubbed it between his palms.

"You see?" he said, on returning. "It's a kind of lichen. Now they can kill it by dusting with chemicals from aircraft. It used to destroy whole forests. Have you ever seen a whole tree-stump covered with down? In summer? It's the stub, the gnawed remnants of the tree, eaten away by the lichen."

"You're fond of the forest?" I asked. "Or do you prefer the steppe? Or perhaps the mountains?"

"I used to love the forest . . ." screwing up his eyes he gazed round at the moon, the snow-drifts, at the dark branches of the firs, unlit by the moon, gazed with satisfaction, slowly, as though drawing at a cigarette . . . "I used to love the mountains too."

"And now?"

He didn't reply.

"It looks as though it's already time to go home," he said. "They give me mustard plasters before I go to bed."

We turned back.

"I love the forest more than anything, even now," I said. "Not as it is now and not at night, but a pine forest on a sunny day. A pine forest has a lot of sky, the trees are sparse and the sky is not only overhead, it's everywhere, wherever one looks. It seems to me the very sky, and not the pines, smells of resin."

He kept silent. We entered a dark stretch and I couldn't see his face.

"One lives in town, for ever sitting at a desk and one doesn't see either the forest or the sky," I complained, becoming more talkative. "Our work is like that. It is difficult to imagine how beautiful life would be if all our work were in a forest . . . or by the sea, or in the mountains . . . if the words we write were born of oxygen . . . if the paper smelled of pine needles . . . if, as one worked, red boulders or red pines were all around . . . as Tolstoy said; 'if you glance around you see nothing but mountains . . . if you raise your head, mountains again . . .' Just imagine, if you raise your head from the page you see mountains . . ."

"And you, have you ever worked in the mountains?"

His step did not falter. His arm guided mine just as firmly. But his voice changed. It became as unadulteratedly clear and sincere as when he asked the journalist whether that editor had kept his job. . . . It was his voice, real and without pretence.

"Have you ever worked in the mountains?" he repeated. "I don't expect you have. But I have, for years. There may be forest all round but not much oxygen. Of course, it was no choice of mine. I was in a concentration camp. A mine. Workers, non-prisoners were in the upper levels, but we were right in the depths, nine or ten levels down. They had electrically powered trucks. There's mechanization for you! But we hauled everything back by hand. They had mechanical cutters. We did our hewing by pick, the old-fashioned way. They worked six hours, we did twelve hours. They ate like normal human beings. We were given 400 grams of bread a day, no more. If we didn't complete our norm, we'd get two hundred. If it happened again, a hundred . . . and so on to nothing . . . A vicious circle, or, to be more precise, fatal. The less you got, the less you could work, the less you worked, the less you got . . . That's nothing. Some ate corpses. They'd cut off a muscle and cook it . . . Watch out, there's a branch."

He helped me to step over the branch which lay across the path and led me on again at a steady, walking pace.

43

I was afraid that he would suddenly stop and say no more. And the door to Alyosha's fate would slam shut again. I waited for his voice, for a word, without seeing either the moon or the trees . . . He was the first messenger from there! I wanted to hurry him, to jog his arm. Please, don't be silent. You are a messenger. I am listening. Don't be silent!

"And the children! There were even children there, too, born there. Some couldn't walk until they were four years old, others at five even hadn't learnt to talk. Their little hands and legs were not like ordinary children's. And we grown-ups too, scarcely looked like human beings. We had abscesses and diarrhoea from hunger. How many I buried there! Amongst them Sasha. For three years I was in charge of a burial party. Sasha Sokolyansky was my friend, almost like a brother. At one time in the Civil War we were partisans together and afterwards in prison. But for him I wouldn't have survived. However much they tortured him he wouldn't give evidence against me . . . Thanks to him I only got five years. He was handsome, kindness itself, a giant of a man, only he stammered a little . . . He began to stammer after the investigation. But even in him this stammer seemed somehow pleasant and childlike. I shared my bread rations with him. I used to cook mushrooms for him in a broken old pot. Many people got poisoned, especially the non-Russians. They didn't know the first thing about mushrooms, they'd never been near a forest. They used to cook up toadstools—and that was the end of them. As for me, I spent years in the woods. And from my partisan days I've learnt to know all about mushrooms and herbs. I tried to cure Sasha with a herbal brew . . . but all to no avail . . . I tied the tag on his leg with my own hands and buried him myself. Not in the common pit but in a separate grave under an old fir-tree like that one and I cut out a mark on the bark."

I looked at the trunk which was lit up by the moon, searching for a mark on it.

The path came to an end. We came out onto the road.

"My husband died there," I said. I don't know where, I don't know from what or when. He was a scientist, a blood specialist. A doctor. What I was told officially was: 'Ten years without right of correspondence', and now it's twelve years and there's no news. Perhaps you buried him too, your party . . ."

We stood on the road under a lamp and gazed at one another. A street lamp is not the moon. There is nothing mysterious about its light. Once again the wrinkles, the hollows and furrows on his large, broad-browed face became visible. The marks were not pockmarks, but scars left by boils . . . Half turning away he brushed the snow of the collar of his coat.

In thirty-seven?" he asked.

"Yes, with confiscation of property.* They came for me, too, later, but I managed to get away. I left my daughter with relatives and went off. I came back when wives were no longer being picked up . . . You haven't come across . . . you don't know . . ." I ventured, "where such special camps—without right of correspondence— were situated?"

"No," he replied quickly, "I haven't come across any such."

Either he didn't want to talk any more or perhaps he had noticed someone else nearby.

We walked to the house. Ahead of us a man was slowly sauntering along.

"Well, have you weighed yourself today?" asked Bilibin, in a loud voice, addressing a fat man who was standing near the clothes-stand, unravelling his scarf and wheezing heavily. "Just imagine, Nina Sergeyevna, Ilya Isaakovich weighs himself every day to see if he hasn't at long last lost some weight. Well, what did the scales show? Any success today? Five kilos? Less?"

There seemed no end to the scarf. The fat man smiled a shy smile. Even his moustache seemed to smile shyly.

"Thank you, Nina Sergeyevna, for the walk and for putting up with a boring old man," Bilibin intoned in his velvety voice, and I went off to my room.

. . . Now I will go to bed. It was quiet and warm in my room. I could not see the little fir-tree through my window. It was pitch dark. And even if I could have seen it it would not have given me back by peace of mind.

It was the first news of Alyosha—and what news! Even if Sasha Sokolyansky was not like him, he was still Alyosha. Soup of toadstools. Common graves as in Leningrad during the blockade.** Had someone made a mark on that pine-tree? Would I ever see it?

The power-station kept ticking. Where would Bilibin be just now? What would he be doing? Would he be smoking? Playing chess with Ilya Isaakovich? Telling amusing war stories in the guest-room? Or perhaps playing billiards with the dark-eyed lady, who had just learned how to pot the balls to show off her supple waist to advantage. "You know you've really blossomed out here," Bilibin would say to her in his velvety voice, "there are flowers which bloom in winter."

"All this was false, only I knew his real voice," I thought, nuzzling my cheek against the pillow.

This morning there was no more snow on the trees. It had melted. From the window the hill seemed unprepossessing, dappled, mottled. Some cows look like that. The fir-tree on the hill had lost its majesty. But when I went along the road to the village, having contrived to breakfast before the others and escape for a walk on my own, I realized that it was good to be in the country in the thaw, to feel as free as the air. A warm wind clung to my cheeks. I took off my gloves, and the wind caressingly touched my fingers. I liked its gentle touch and avoided the grove so as not to part company with it. In the deep tracks of the Bykovo road the blue sky was reflected in the ruffled water of the puddles, and clouds floated over the sky like little paper ships. The warm wind frolicked over road and field and flew off to tumble the sodden birch-trees which stood perkily in little families on the other side of the ravine. The thought of the wind tearing drops of water from the branches and the drops running down the back of my neck sent a shudder down between my shoulder blades. I walked as far as the sodden hay-rick and turned back, not knowing which way to go. If you had picked up the hay-rick, put your arms round it and squeezed, the water would have run out from it as from a sponge. The wind had tired me. I remembered the pale blue bench on one of the paths near the house and walked over to it. But the seat was occupied.

It was Veksler, the grey-haired Jewish poet with his war-decorations, sitting on a newspaper he had spread out. I had heard that during the war he had fought in these parts. The wind ruffled some papers lying next to him on the bench. From the way I had walked up it was quite clear that I intended to sit down for a while, so the poet jumped up and with his small red hands began hurriedly to clear away the papers to free a place for me. Of course I was disturbing him, but it would have been impolite to have gone by after he had made such hasty, well-intentioned preparations.

He had young, quick eyes, distinctive grey hair and the narrow sunken mouth of an old man. Age and youth were plainly struggling for mastery in that face.

"Those are my poems," he explained at once, noticing that I was watching him hastily trying to stuff the papers into the inside pocket of his jacket. "Rather, translations of my poems."

"You were obviously working and I've hindered you," I said. I liked the way his hands trembled as they touched the sheets. "Please do read a little if it is not too difficult for you to read here, in the open. I love poetry."

He looked at me dubiously, wondering how on earth he could read to someone he didn't know just like that, but he took out the papers. His lips moved like an old man's. A youthful spark gleamed in his eyes. He unfolded one sheet.

"No, read it to me first in Yiddish, then tell it to me in Russian, and only then read me the verse translation," I said. "Then I shall understand better."

He moved his lips again. He obviously wanted to read, but he examined my face wondering if it was worth it.

However, he began. The ageing shape of his mouth changed. There remained the fearless eyes of a man who had resolved on the bold action of telling a stranger about himself. He read in Yiddish. The language, which had always seemed to me ugly, in this reading was magnificent, as no doubt any language is when heard in harmony and not in chaos.

Hesitating, unable to find the right words, he started to retell me in Russian what he had already read and I again saw the sunken mouth and the fingers which had turned blue.

They were poems about war. About the night of the commanding-officer, a communist, who had to send into battle at dawn the next morning eighteen-year-olds just arrived at the front. He knew that somewhere on another sector of the front another commanding-officer, just as advanced in years and a communist like himself—would send into battle his own eighteen-year-old son on the very same morning . . . Whilst telling the story, trying to find the right words, Veksler, without noticing it, got up. I, too, rose with him and we followed a wet track across the field to the village.

He spoke—rephrasing his verses in prose—about the profound darkness before dawn and about the faces of those asleep, and how boyish foreheads, necks, brows and cheekbones cut through the darkness of dawn. The commander involuntarily sought out amongst those faces his own son's, although he knew that his son was hundreds of kilometres away. I avoided the puddles, but Veksler, in his excitement, jumped over them lightly and awkwardly. He would speak a line in Yiddish, then grope for the Russian words. Again I found myself by the browny-green, sodden rick. The boys were drawn up, and the commanding officer peered into their faces and tried to guess the fate of each soldier and of his own son, far away. Veksler saw that the story had touched me and it was probably this that made his hand shake as he lit a cigarette, turning away against the wind.

"The night can be heard in your verses," I said, "and the bitterness of the evening before. And even the son's features show through the strangers' faces. It's good, very good, as far as I can judge from the sound of the original and from your account. And now please read the translation."

He pulled out the sheets. Oh, how ugly our language can be, how harshly words can be thrust into lines! How unwilling they may be to stand side by side! They seem to want to stick out in all directions! There was neither the night, nor desperation, nor hope, nor the boyish sleeping faces—just awkward lines. Merely words thrust into metre and not the night, or the faces, or the evening before, not the distance between him and his son, or sorrow. We could already see the roofs of the little houses of Bykovo. A woman, wet through, in men's boots and a dirty shawl, was coming towards us with a long switch. Looking at her angular, wet face it seemed that there would never be sunshine or fine weather. There would never be snow, there would never be books or the warmth of a room. And there would be no need for any poetry.

I took from his hands a sheet and began to read myself, explaining to him the ugliness and weakness of each line of the translation. We turned back. He was nervously smoking. I tried to make him understand the aridity of this text, the futility of being exact and to make him hear the lifeless beat of the words.

"How you can talk about poetry!" he said, thoughtfully, and again moved his lips. "You write yourself, I suppose."

"No," I lied. "I just love reading it."

"And you've never written any?"

"Never."

He stood for a moment.

"I would like an editor like that," he said in a business-like way. "An editor like you. My poems will appear in

*Emes** in Yiddish, in *Novy Mir** and in *Znamya** in Russian. I can hear myself that the translation doesn't come off, but I can't explain why. I don't know Russian well enough. Do you see that grave?" he interrupted himself. "On this very spot my friend, Lieutenant Koptyaev, died and was buried here. I come here every day."

We jumped across a little ditch and stood by the fence. Everywhere there were graves, wherever you looked. At first you scarcely noticed them. They revealed their rounded spines and triangular obelisks from behind the trunks of birch-trees or from under your feet in the open field. This grave had been enclosed by a wooden fence painted a pale blue colour like the railings of the bridge over the stream or like the arbour in the grove of oak trees near the house. That is why, looking at it a long way off, I had not recognized it as a grave. Inside the fence there was a small wooden triangle of the same pale blue colour.

My new friend took off his hat. His face beneath the grey hairs blown by the wind became solemn. I began to feel awkward. Knitting my brows, I tried to imagine the whistle of bullets, the earth under one's knees, one's stomach and chest, to imagine this village, seen from below, from the ground-level, and the rattle of machine-guns, but I didn't succeed. I only saw a little pale blue fence, and a slightly ridiculous man, prematurely aged, with a tense face.

"Where was Alyosha's grave?" I asked myself as I always did in front of every grave-mound. "There . . . where Bilibin had described, in the mountains? Or in the forest . . . And was there a little mound there?"

I thought how age had changed me. In my childhood and youth I had been certain that graves were unnecessary. But now it seemed to me that the most important thing in my life was to find Alyosha's grave.

"What's the matter? Let's go!" Veksler said in alarm, as though he had overheard my thoughts. We were walking along next to one another and he kept glancing at me sideways, turning his neck in a quick bird-like movement.

"Tell me what it was like fighting here," I asked, to avoid his guessing anything. What if he suddenly looked at me more intently and saw what was within?

He started to tell me where the artillery had been positioned, where the infantry had attacked from, about the attacks and reconnaissance. He spoke with an accent, unsure of his stresses. I listened very attentively, following his finger with my eyes, closely observing the hills and groves, but understanding absolutely nothing. Not, of course on account of his accent, but because of my insensitivity to figures and topography. He talked of kilometres, of the numbers of units and military operations. I kept nodding. And of Stalin's plan for the annihilation of the Germans outside Moscow, the utter brilliance of which he had only recently become aware of.

"I lost my son," he said, finally. This I had understood. "On the Ukrainian front. He was eighteen years old. Just at the time when we were engaged at Bykovo here."

"Your only son?"

"Yes, Lyutik. My wife thought up the name. You know that it's the name of a flower."

We walked to the house.

"Will you listen to some more of my poetry sometime?" he asked, as we were wiping our dirty feet on the wire mat in the entrance.

"Yes, I will. Of course."

The guest-room resounded with the radio, animated voices and the banging of dominoes on the table. The quiet of my room, the neatly-made bed and the dark tree through the window welcomed me, but the anxiety which I felt since yesterday had not abated.

I hadn't seen Bilibin since our conversation of the previous day. In what tone of voice would he speak to me now? I listened to the melodic chimes of the clock in the guest-room as I waited for lunch. Everything put me off reading: my wrist-watch, footsteps along the corridor, and the distant voices. Everything increased my anxiety.

"Lunch is served!" said Lyudmila Pavlovna at last, in a discreet but loud voice from somewhere near the door.

The film director was sitting in the deserted guest-room gazing unblinkingly at the radio as though at a fire in the hearth.

"The pernicious activity of the progeny of bourgeois aestheticism," I heard, "who have built themselves a cosy nest in the offices of Leningrad's theatrical society,* has been completely exposed."

The portly gentleman, suffering from high blood-pressure, was also coming down the stairs. I saw a shiver suddenly run through him, his shoulders writhed (as though cold water had dripped down the back of his neck) and this shudder involuntarily communicated itself to me. I don't know what affected him, but it was the words "have built themselves a cosy nest" that made me shiver . . . I felt the breath of 1937 upon me . . . But I could not properly make out who on this occasion had made themselves a 'cosy nest', and where.

Bilibin and Sergei Dimitriyevich were already sitting at their places. Bilibin got up, greeted me, moved my chair back and sat down again.

"Been for a walk?" he asked amiably. "Ah, youth, youth . . . I advise you to start with this salad . . . you're not an old 'un like me. I spend more and more time sitting in my own room."

I stared at him with wide open eyes. It was just as though there had been no yesterday evening! He talked to me in the same way as he had done before.

"What aesthetic critics exactly were they talking about on the radio today?" I asked. "I didn't quite get it."

"About theatre critics," Sergei Dimitreyevich replied, frowning. "They've winkled out some group or other . . . You know how it is with us, they like to lay it on thick. I think it's all grossly exaggerated. There are real Marxists, genuine connoisseurs of the theatre amongst the theatre critics. I don't see anything vicious in their articles. Zelenin, Samoilov . . . they're knowledgeable, talented people. And it's they who have taken the blow. It's disgusting!"

Bilibin moved the salad-bowl over to my plate. "May I?" and helped me to a spoonful.

Sergei Dimitriyevich wanted to add something in his indignation, but Bilibin interrupted him.

"We had a cook in our regiment," he said hastily, tucking his serviette into his collar. "He was a pure artist, a magician . . . One day something mysterious was dished up on my plate. I smelled it. It was good. I tasted it. It was good, but I couldn't make out what it was. I said; 'What are you giving me to eat today, old man?' 'That, comrade major, was hedgehog,' he replied."

Sergei Dimitriyevich burst into loud laughter, but it didn't make me laugh.

"It was hedgehog," repeated Bilibin, looking at me with his yellow eyes.

Today I saw a striking fir-tree in the grove. How had I missed it before? It stood, magnificent, mighty, in a tight circle of birch-trees. A prisoner. A happy prisoner. When I saw it I laughed out loud. The birch trees like little girls decked out in their finery were dancing round the Christmas tree. All their lives they had been celebrating Christmas Eve. Today it was grey, so grey and swampy in the grove. A grey-blue slush lay beneath my feet. But here in the open air even the slush had a silvery beauty. It seemed a pity to trample on it. Looking round I saw that I was quite alone and I began to recite some poetry. I tried to fit the sounds to the birch-trees, to this treacherous snow.

I tried out Pushkin, Pasternak, Nekrasov and Akhmatova. Yes, they were all from here. They all fitted in. "All Correct", as one would say in checking a telegram . . . All the words grew from this soil, and drawing in a deep breath, stretched upwards to the sky like the birch-trees. As I recited the poetry I felt not only its beauty but also its lassitude and its joy in itself. My lips were happy to meet the words and the words my lips.

> The snow storm fiercely howled
> And flung the snow against the panes.
> The sun was rising sombrely.
> That morning it looked out upon
> The sadness of the scene.*

When I was a child did I not weep over every line of 'Red-Nosed Frost' because it was pure music, pure streams of music? To take the ordinary words "flung the snow against the panes" and create a symphony from them!

I heard voices behind me and I lapsed into silence.

Probably somebody had also heard me—people always overheard me when I read poetry to myself and it always amused them . . . The journalist and his wife were walking behind me and caught me up.

She had come to stay with him for three days. I had already seen her today but not close to. She was a tall, strong woman, probably beautiful, if by beauty one means shapely legs and a firm, shapely waist. Beside the narrow-shouldered journalist in his spectacles she seemed particularly well built and strong with her white teeth. There was nowhere where I could turn off so we walked on together. My joy faded, the walk was spoiled. Further on in Nekrasov's poem there are such gems! I was afraid of strangers and disliked them and always became aware of them at once.

"Was it you reading poetry?" the journalist's wife asked.

"Me."

"Who were you reading it to?" she persisted, without shortening her quick, brisk steps and leading the way.

"To myself," I said. "Who else would I be reading to?"

The journalist plodded clumsily behind us. Since I had seen his face there on the bridge I had almost believed that the fur collar and the fancy knob had no special meaning and were not so directly connected with him. But now, seeing the wife's well-proportioned figure, the handbag slung over her shoulder and hearing her voice and laughter I thought "No, both the fur collar and the knob were not accidental. They had a meaning."

His wife stopped for a moment, took a handful of sunflower seeds from her pocket and offered them to me on the palm of her hand.

"Do you want some?"

"No, thank you. If one opens them with one's nails one's hands freeze and I cannot do it with my teeth."

"Can't you? It's fun to do it with your mouth. And then spit out the husks as far as you can!" Laughing, she spat a whole heap onto the path in front of her. Two or three black husks stuck to the trunk of a birch-tree.

"Whose poetry were you reciting?" she enquired. "Yesenin?"*

"No, why should it be Yesenin? Pushkin, Pasternak and Nekrasov."

"Pasternak is very obscure. Recently Seryozha and I were reading—do you remember, Sergei, at the Stepanovs'? Everyone split their sides laughing. You couldn't understand a thing."

I looked round at the journalist. He was walking along, hunching his shoulders timidly. He needn't have been afraid; I had no intention of arguing.

"But what a revealing thing one's wife is," I thought, as I walked behind her shapely hips and watched her happily spitting. The words "It's fun to do it with your mouth" appears to him to be wit; the carthorse strength and lightness of step—beauty; and that stupid laugh—candour. In her spitting he sees something spontaneous, childlike maybe, and intimacy with ordinary people.

We went into the house. His wife watched carefully to see where and how the coats were hung, and the boots and the stick. I went to my room.

Bilibin was wandering up and down the corridor alone, smoking.

"Been out for a walk?" he asked in his beautiful velvety tones. "You have roses on your cheeks." Why did he talk to me like that? After the forest! And after that evening!

He guessed at once that he had struck the wrong note

and stopped smiling.

"Let's go out after tea. I'll knock on your door. May I?" he asked, throwing away the cigarette just as he had the smile.

"Of course."

I was in a hurry to take a bath. What a delight a warm bath was after the cold of the air; there were the shining tiles, the dull reflection of the lines of one's own body, engulfed by the scent of pine needles and resilient water! If, in addition, there had been peace the delight would have been complete.

But no, in the next cubicle, which was divided from mine by a grey, quivering piece of linen I heard the voice of the dark-eyed lady—Valentina Nikolayevna. Not her ordinary voice but a sweet little voice.

"Have I much longer?" She slapped the water with the palms of her hands. "And if I don't want any longer?"

It made me laugh. I knew at once from her voice that she was not saying it for my benefit nor for Galya's—the bath attendant. Why should she act as though she was a frail, playful, splashing child?

Indeed, from somewhere, not so far away, came a deep cough. It sounded like the film director.

Two writers of adventure stories were taking a bath in two neighbouring cubicles, one in the cubicle next to me and the other in the last one in our row. One of them writes science fiction. The other simply adventure stories. I had often seen them in the drawing-room, deep in thought over a chess-board.

"Have you got an 'Olympia'?" one of them asked.

"No, a 'Crown'—in the new series. It's a portable."

There was silence. Some wheezing. The splashing of water.

"And how many pages do you do a day?" enquired the writer of adventure stories only.

"Well, that depends," the science fictionist replied. . . . "If it's descriptions of nature one can do fifteen to twenty . . . If it's character psychology, then it goes quickly. But if it's a case of something technical then, of course, it's slower and more difficult."

They stopped talking. They were considering a fresh problem from the realms of literary theory.

I heard some gurgling sounds from Valentina Nikolayevna's cubicle. She had evidently turned the tap on and was letting water into the bath.

"It's not permitted to fill up with hot water. The doctor doesn't allow it. You can have as much cold as you like," Galya said sternly.

"But what if I like hot water?" said Valentina Nikolayevna and went on splashing around. "Let the doctor take a bath in cold water himself. I like it hotter. I'm like that. I like everything hot."

I could hardly refrain from laughing. I knew that Valentina Nikolayevna, who had been an employee in the Writers' Union (she had worked in the personnel department), had recently married the Stalin Prize Winner, Zaborov. He was at that moment discussing final arrangements with his previous wife as to who should get the dacha and who the flat; when he had reached an agreement he would come to fetch Valentina Nikolayevna. In the meantime she was taking a cure and turning the heads of the adventure story writers and the film director. On her account they had already swapped chess for billiards; and the science fictionist had already promised to portray her as the woman of the future in his novel.

"I love everything hot," Valentina Nikolayevna repeated.

The story writers, however, were busy with literary problems and didn't respond to her advances. Only Lado put in a word. I couldn't hear what he said, but Valentina Nikolayevna gleefully shouted "Oh, you naughty man," giving the phrase a French intonation.

"Well, and when you finish a manuscript," the adventure writer pursued his questioning, "do you show it to someone or hand it straight to the publishers? To some literary critic or other?"

"Not to anyone," the science fictionist replied bluntly. "I assure you they're all aesthetes, down to the last man. The mass reader is another question . . . I test it at once on the mass audience."

"I show mine to my wife," said the adventure writer. "She didn't study in any of those institutions but she has a natural perfect taste."

I went back to my room. Outside the window the snow-storm was painting the air, my little fir-tree on the hill and no doubt that fir-tree in the forest which was prisoner of the birch-trees. The deliberate strokes fell in one direction, always in one and the same direction.

"It's a good thing it's snow and not slush," I thought. "It will be nice for us to walk in the snow."

I lay down after the bath, and at once fell asleep. When I woke up the snowstorm had abated and outside my window the sunset was glowing pink in its usual place. Soon, it too would darken. Then the time would come for us to set out.

I didn't go down to tea. I sat down at the table to read and wait. And since I was certain that he would come without fail I found it easy to wait. What I was reading was interesting. And I listened to the footsteps in the corridor. The one occupation did not interfere at all with the other.

He would come here to this room, and would at once become what he had been in the forest. He would tell me more and more about that other life. He was a 'messenger! How had he been able—how had he found the strength—to survive it? I would ask him what had helped him to bear it.

There were lots of footsteps, but none of them were his. I was amazed to find that I was so familiar with the sound of his footsteps: heavy; yet agile and in some way smooth.

Once I thought—those must be his steps. A board right by the door squeaked and my heart sank at the sound. Were they coming here? No, they went by.

I felt ashamed that my heart had sunk.

I took my muff, gloves, scarf and went downstairs to put on my things. I would go alone. Evidently, he didn't want to continue the story or he had simply forgotten our understanding . . . Well, that was understandable. Stories like that were not cheerful.

On my way I glanced in the drawing-room to see if he was perhaps there. He wasn't. I took two or three steps down the stairs and, all of a sudden, to my own surprise, turned round and walked down the corridor to room No. 8. . . .

All the doors were the same. I peered at the numbers: 4, 5, 6. Ah, there was 8.

I knocked.

There was no answer.

Perhaps it was the wrong number? I stepped back a pace, raised my head and looked . . . Yes, it was the right one.

I knocked again.

There was no reply.

But from inside I heard an odd noise.

I pushed the door and entered.

Bilibin, fully dressed, was lying heavily on top of the bedcover on a wide, low bed. The bedside lamp seemed to cast moonlight on his face and broad chest. When I came closer I saw that his eyes were wide open and staring at me. One arm hung down from the bed. When I approached and stood over him he didn't move. It might have been my fancy but he seemed to be looking not at me but simply in front of him. His eyes seemed motionless and black.

No, he was looking at me. Without moving his head, his eyes followed mine as I approached still closer to the bed.

"Are you unwell?"

His blue lips seemed to quiver. He said something to me and mouthed several words but I couldn't catch what. He even smiled—it seemed to me ironically. And because he had tried hard to say something to me with his lips and eyes whilst remaining completely immobile, and because he was unsuccessful in his attempt, I was more frightened than if he had groaned.

And that lamp casting its moonlight on his face and hand!

I took his heavy arm and, bending it carefully, placed it on his chest. I was frightened at my own movement. It was thus one folds the arms of the dead.

I rushed downstairs to the doctor in the duty office. I found both the doctor and a nurse. I gathered by the way they both chased up the stairs at my words that they were much better informed about his illness than I.

"Why's his bell out of order?" said the doctor to the nurse as they rushed off. "It would be his bell."

I settled down in the drawing-room to wait. There I was with my muff on my knees waiting for the doctor to emerge. The sister rushed out and then returned—still running—with a metal box, some ampoules and a syringe and I was still sitting there, waiting for the doctor to come out.

After a pause, the radio announcer continued:

"Zelenin (Zelikson) casts a slur on Soviet drama in alleging that it presents history in an effete and watered down way. Soviet literature, with its alleged primitivism, doesn't suit these subtle aesthetes."

The speaker prevented me from listening to the sounds coming from the room opposite but it didn't occur to me to switch the radio off, and I sat mechanically tracing on my muff with my finger shorthand symbols of ready-made phrases. "These disciples of decadent eccentricity find Soviet patriotism and the principles of Soviet realism unpalatable," the speaker went on.

The words 'decadent eccentricity' would, I supposed, have to be written separately. This formula had not been used before.

At length the doctor came out of the room.

"Is it very bad?"

"An attack of angina. The bell was out of order. It was lucky for him that you looked in just at that moment. It could have been much worse . . . We've injected some camphor and coramine. Now he just needs rest. Nurse will stay with him and I'll send up the electrician. You can pay him a visit if you like in the evening, but on condition that you don't let him talk too much."

"No, I won't. I shall only ask him what he was trying to say when I went in."

I returned to my room. At last I got rid of my muff, gloves and scarf and went down to supper.

Sergei Dimitriyevich and his wife were sitting at my table. "What's happened to our neighbour? I hear that he's been taken ill, poor man. If you visit him give him my best wishes." "And mine," said his wife. "I've already confessed to Sergei that I've taken a fancy to him! He polishes his nails. He's got such style. And what a beautiful forehead! I really have fallen for your writer."

Sergei Dimitriyevich told me that unfortunately he personally couldn't visit the sick man as he and his wife were leaving in an hour's time for Moscow.

"Why's that? I thought you had no intention of leaving."

"Well, you know . . . there's an editorial meeting . . . My wife says it's awkward. I ought to speak even though I'm on leave. The editor won't like it if I say nothing."

"A meeting about what?"

"Oh, about our cosmopolitan mistakes. Of course, some people do lay it on too thick, but one must admit there have been some cosmopolitan mistakes. Particularly in our department."

At nine o'clock I knocked again on Bilibin's door. "Come in!" came the nurse's voice.

He was without his jacket, lying under a blanket which covered him to the waist. His white shirt made his broad chest appear even broader. The lamp now lit up a different face, no longer grey and blue-lipped. His eyes looked peaceful and sharp like a hawk's.

He was glad to see me and asked me to take a seat.

"Would you take a turn at looking after our patient and I'll pop down for some supper," said the nurse leaving us. "If anything happens, press the bell."

"I've got angina," said Nikolai Aleksandrovich in a rather hollow voice. "It certainly caught me. If it weren't for you I would be in the next world now. One used to say 'my number's up', now it's called 'coronary'. It's the second already. And there was nitroglycerine by my side, but I couldn't move . . ."

"What did you say to me when I came in? What did you want to say?"

"That's what work in the mountains reduces you to," he said slowly almost syllable by syllable.

We looked at one another again as we had on the footpath in the forest, directly without lowering our eyes.

. . . February 1949

Today it was still snowing and the snowstorm had a touchingly preoccupied look about it. It was whirling and whirling and covering up its tracks, as though blessing the houses, fir-trees and us and saying: "Sleep, my dears, don't worry, it will all pass, it's all just nonsence . . ."

The grove was no longer like a crystal, but soft, cosy, spreading, downy. It was all covered in magnificent fluffed-up drifts.

The deep path, strewn with soft powdery snow was quite untouched and I trod sparingly and carefully. I was the first. The snow wrapped the heart, like the path in something soft. I thrust aside and threw out the thorns from my heart: the newspaper rubbish about cosmopolitans, the memory of Elizaveta Nikolayevna, whose voice still polluted the very air around Katya. Peace from this unsparkling, soft, powdery whiteness filled my heart.

Early in the morning, whilst everyone was still asleep, I gently made the descent below the waters and worked for a long time. It was now more difficult not to write than to write. My memory, obligingly presented me with faces, voices and moments. Then, after breakfast, I set off for the grove. I had been writing about something terrible, but walking I found easy today; probably because I knew that Bilibin was lying in room No. 8 and waiting for me. He was waiting, but I would not be coming all that soon. The grove was filled to the brim with his waiting and as I picked my way along the path I could hear the passing of the minutes which he was counting off in his room. What did I see in this man? What was he to me? I didn't know. But I didn't doubt that he felt my absence in the hours I spent in the grove and for that reason it was enticing today and so pleasant to wander; and to think, but not of him, and not even of the news from the other world.

I stopped to look at the birch-trees. They stood in a greyish haze and at the top the grey was delicately tinged with pink. I examined the sky—perhaps somewhere the dawn was still brightly shining? No, how could it turn up here in broad daylight! I remembered Blok's words:

All at once there lights up that circle
High above you, obscure, which I saw
In the past with its grey and its purple.*

I always wondered when I read those lines why grey and purple? Where did they come from? Does grey and purple really happen in nature? But today I had seen the grey tops of the birch-trees growing pink.

This set me off thinking about Blok, not about his Russian birch-trees, but about the Russian path his life took, along which he encountered all our great writers—Tolstoy, Dostoevsky, Nekrasov and Gogol—about that path which in Russia casts the poet down from the skies of poetry to the moral reality of earth. In the distance beyond the horizon those skies and that earth meet . . . There, grief acquires music and song truth.

Not without cause does the insulted genius
Each generation praise . . .

Like he, they all are wounded in their hearts,
Their singing hearts . . .

wrote Blok.

I plunge down from the skies of poetry into
communism,
Just because I have no love without it.

wrote Mayakovsky,* the grievously insulted genius of the next generation. "Communism" meant justice to him, and without justice there could be no love, no art, not even breath itself. Their paths were similar like almost all Russian paths and their deaths were similar. The earth, onto which both of them had flung themselves from the skies of poetry, had yawned beneath them and swallowed them up.

I glanced once again at the birch-trees. The grey had grown deeper and the pink had faded.

Back home in my room I sat for a little while next to the pipes of the central heating and thawed out my hands and feet. Then I went to see Bilibin.

On leaving my room I came face to face with Veksler. I didn't like the embarrassed, even slightly pathetic smile with which he greeted me.

"Well, how are things?" he asked. "Why haven't you been around? Are you off for a walk?"

"No," I replied, "I've just come back. I'm on my way to visit Nikolai Aleksandrovich."

"May I come with you?"

"I'm going to listen to something he wouldn't say in your presence!" was what I wanted to reply. "I'm going to listen to news from *over there*, news from another planet about Alyosha. What has it got to do with you? It was *me* Bilibin trusted. He doesn't know you."

"The doctor said that he should only have one visitor at a time, so as not to tire him," I invented. "Did you know that he had a serious heart attack? He may have coronary thrombosis—and it would be the second. I'll stay with him now for a while and you call in before supper."

Veksler, looking small and old, retreated with what might have been an inclination of the head or a shrug of the shoulders.

I knocked.

Bilibin was sitting up in bed, propped up by large pillows.

"Greetings!" he boomed. "So you've remembered your twin-neighbour and come to visit him at last? Well, what was it like today, was there any mousse for sweet? I don't get any. 'Gelatine is bad for you,' they say. If you believe the doctors you'll die of hunger."

I didn't say anything and waited for the conventional note to die away.

"Tell me, was it there you contracted heart disease?" I asked.

"Yes, there. The actual coronary happened later, in the war, but it all began there. You should have seen me before. I was as strong as a horse."

"And you spent the whole five years working in the mine?"

"No, the first two I was felling trees," he said, casting an anxious look towards the door and then, for some reason or other, at the ceiling. "At first it was the forest, then two years later, the mine. The war saved me. They put me in the army and I got as far as Berlin."

Then he went on talking in a whisper. Not about Berlin and not about Moo-Moo 2.

He could not have often had the chance of talking about camp life because he spoke with the same insatiable voraciousness with which I listened to him.

68

It wasn't a coherent story but like some kind of spots wandering around his memory, working to the surface and making a notch in mine at the same time.

The cattle-truck. For days on end people travelled standing. The dead would fall on the shoulders of the living.

In the transit camps—they were still in Moscow—there was a notorious guard. He used to amuse himself by preventing the prisoners from sleeping. He would jog somebody's shoulder at night, wake him up and make him pick up a cigarette-butt from the floor. Or would simply bark something into his ears. Just for the hell of it. For no particular reason. To enjoy watching the person jump.

There was another incident. Bilibin was working at the time in the forest. They had already been lined up in the morning ready to be led off. They were guarded by soldiers and dogs. Alsatians. The dogs were trained to fling themselves on anybody taking a single step outside the ranks of the column. A prisoner—as far as I remember he came from Leningrad—had had a letter from his wife the day before. And probably hadn't had time to read it in the barracks, or he wanted to reread it. I'm not sure which. He surreptitiously took the letter from his pocket and started to read it when they were already lined up. The wind suddenly tore it from his hands and carried it off. He ran after it, breaking ranks. A dog jumped on him and tore him to bits.

Bilibin stopped. I was silent too. He grew tired of sitting, lay down and stretched himself out to his full length on the bed.

"It's a good thing I didn't know Alyosha's address," I said. "Without right of correspondence he would never have been able to drop my piece of paper. A dog could never have torn him to pieces on my account."

"Draw your chair up closer," Bilibin suddenly said. I drew it up. His head buried itself deeper in the pillows. I leant over. Hastily and harshly, fearing to cause me pain but overcoming this fear by his harshness, Bilibin explained—he even spoke in a kind of business-like tone that I had the wrong idea about Alyosha's end. He was never taken anywhere, he had never suffered from cattle-trucks or dogs. Everything was over long before that. According to Nikolai Aleksandrovich "ten years without right of correspondence" simply meant execution by firing squad. To avoid repeating at the windows 'exe-cuted', 'executed' and so that there should be no howling and crying in the queue.

"We were never allowed to write very often wherever we were," he said. "But special camps with 'ten years without right of correspondence' just never existed. And there were no such sentences. I can guarantee you that."

He closed his eyes.

"It's better that way," I said. "Without Alsatians. In any case he wouldn't have survived there. He was a very strong man and fearless, but not fitted . . . for . . . felling trees. Strong and yet weak."

Bilibin didn't speak.

I don't know what he could see in his mind but I saw the wall, Alyosha's last steps and the squad of soldiers, awaiting the command.

Did it happen in the middle of the night? Or during that day, when the sun was shining? Where had I been at that moment? Had I been with him in my thoughts?

Only I think now it's all done quite differently. The soldiers, the wall—that's something out of the nine-teenth century.

Nowadays it was quite different.

Bilibin opened his eyes. He must have read my thoughts, because he said: "It's done all of a sudden. Whilst being led from one place to another. In the back of the neck." Whilst he spoke he pressed his head deep into the pillow. At that moment he probably felt his own neck as I did mine. The shores of the pillow had parted and his face now lay deep in the depths. "That's all there is to it," he said. "All there is."

"Thank you for not sparing me or yourself."

"It doesn't make you cry?"

"No. If you—and others—manage to survive then it doesn't do for me to cry."

"Come tomorrow, a bit earlier."

I gave him my hand. Slowly and with difficulty he raised himself onto his elbow, laboriously turned his bulky form onto its side and took my hand in his. He kissed it, then looked at me and kissed it again.

I left.

. . . March 1949

So they had simply killed him. And all my queueing at that time in Leningrad and Moscow had been to no purpose. All the applications. The letters. The requests for a retrial. All had been too late. Whilst I was still rushing from one office window to another, Alyosha had already been lying a long time under the ground.

Where had they buried him?

Even after killing him they went on lying to me for many years.

"There are no grounds for a retrial."

"When his term is up he'll write to you himself."

"We've no information about his death." And the last

71

time, two years ago; "He may be alive, he may be dead, how should I know? We're not a registry office for such as you. They don't inform us about deaths. Try the registry office."

However strange it may seem, I slept that night. In fact, perhaps it was better for Alyosha to die like that?

The next day proved to be worrying and not conducive to work. It brought with it, as though on a plate, fresh anxieties, both in the paper, which I read at breakfast, and out walking and at home. No going under took place today and the meeting with Bilibin proved empty. Everything was disturbing.

On my way to breakfast I looked in the guest-room for the latest number of the *Literary Gazette* and whilst eating by myself read it through from beginning to end.

The headline of the leading article ran: "Raise the Standard of Bolshevik Party Discipline."

"One must admit that the magazine *Znamya* has lowered the ideological and artistic quality of the material it publishes and has printed a number of ideologically-unhealthy and artistically inferior works with a cosmopolitan taint and formalistic quirks."

There was a report on the meeting of the staff of the *Literary Gazette* and there, amongst other speeches, was the speech of kind, gentle Sergei Dimitriyevich:

"Comrades, I have to admit frankly and in a true Party spirit that only thanks to sharp criticism from the Party press have my eyes at last been opened to the wickedness of the practice of patronage towards one's friends."

The second column was headed "Cosmopolitans in the review *The Theatre*".

"Professor Shumilov (Shneierman), idealist and formalist, inveterate representative of the comparative

72

school, and rabid protagonist of everything foreign, has throughout his life vilely propogated unworthy theories humiliating the dignity of Soviet man and has littered the minds of our young people with anti-scientific dogma."

The third column ran: "A cosmopolitan on a remarkable Soviet actor . . .".

I glanced through the clean windowpane at the little fir-tree and the glittering, sloping cloth of snow as though making the sign of the cross and asking for help and protection. But the words of the articles stabbed the brain like thorns lodged there long ago and now beginning to bite deeper and deeper.

"Worthless ideas," "Shoddy tendencies"—

I had read all that before. And "Raise the standard"— only in those days it was the "standard of vigilance", and "inveterate"—only then it was usually applied to "double-dealer" or "enemy" (the fixed formulae were "raise the standard of Bolshevik vigilance!" and "inveterate double-dealer"). And that hyphen so horridly familiar in the attribute "idealogically-unhealthy", even that hyphen was from those days . . . They were clichés turning somersaults in emptiness.

I had difficulty in swallowing the cottage cheese. I felt that if I took the newspaper back to the guest-room, left it there and went off by myself to the grove to breathe my fill of pure air I would rid my system of the poison, just as one gets rid of poisonous fumes. But, in the grove, encounter followed encounter, each more bitter than the other. The people were all different but they all kept harping on the same thing, as though a stage-director had put them there on purpose to increase my alarm.

A girl whom I often saw in the corridor—I didn't know whether she was a cleaner or a nurse—was walking towards me. She was very young but the perpetual gloomy expression of her face made her look older. A little girl, six or seven years old was mincing and running along in front of her. Nothing the little girl was wearing fitted her. Her clothes were other people's cast-offs. She had on large felt boots, a grease-stained padded jacket with the buttons torn off and a large black shawl fastened cross-wise so that the knot came in front, a little higher than the knees. The shawl kept slipping onto her cheeks and her forehead first on one side, then on the other and however I screwed up my eyes and peered I couldn't make out her face . . . On seeing me both of them, the big girl and the little girl, gave way by stepping into the snow and the little girl sank right in.

"Now buzz off home!" the elder girl ordered the little girl sternly, and quickly strode off along the path to the rest-home. "You've come far enough! Can't you hear me? Go home! Your little Vitka must be howling by now! Off you go. Do you hear me?"

The little girl blinked her eyes, sniffed and tried to brush the shawl off her forehead with her sleeve.

I picked her up under the arms and put her back on the path. She watched the elder girl, striding off amongst the birch-trees.

"Your sister?" I asked, bending down.

"Cousin," replied the little girl, readily. "Our surname's Simakov and she's a Lastochkin."

"And what's your name?"

"Lyolka."

She was still standing there watching the back of her cousin disappearing towards the main building. The little girl's face had a bluish tinge, the colour of skimmed milk.

"Well now, let's get acquainted, Lyolka," I said. "Why do you never come to see us? Where does your cousin

work? She should bring you to our cinema. They sometimes show interesting films."

"In the store . . . We're not supposed to go into the
big house."

She turned and strode back along the path and I
followed her. Wrapped in her black shawl, ungainly,
tottering along in enormous felt boots, she looked like a
small live scarecrow in the snow.

"Why aren't you allowed into the big house?"

Lyolka replied without turning her head as she
walked on:

"It's for writers . . . And we might bring in a lot of
mud. Lyudmila Pavlovna said: 'I'll twist your ears if I
see you!' And Tonka said: 'Don't you come running to
me or they'll throw me out because of you'."

"Where's your mother?"

"She works at the cardboard-box factory. At Zagor-
yanka."

"And your father?"

"Missing."

I stood for a while and watched her as she walked,
black amongst the birch-trees, like a little stump.

"Lyolka, good-bye!" I shouted. She tried to turn
around, but got entangled with her shawl and shouted
ahead instead of to me: "Bye-bye!"

I turned off onto a side path. Fluffy white pillows had
cosily settled themselves on the black branches. Sometimes it was difficult to understand what kept them there,
those slender bare branches and a whole fluffy ball on
the twigs! The ball would perch there, scarcely touching
the branches and would lie there, as if there was nothing
to it. The little fir-trees, warmly wrapped up in snow,
looked like a kindergarten which had been lovingly taken
out for a walk . . . "And we might bring in a lot of mud!"

75

stuck in my gorge like a thorn. I looked with hatred at the stout lady in a fashionable black coat and fluffy shawl who was coming towards me. It was Lyudmila Pavlovna.

"Talk of the Devil! It would be interesting to know if she threw them out of the forest as well," I thought.

Watching her graceful gait, I remembered how she had recently prevented me from working. When everyone had gone to the cinema and a dependable quiet had descended which, I knew, would last about two hours, I sat down at the table 'to make a descent'. And suddenly, when that day which I wished to summon from the past, had clearly presented itself to me, the rattling of door locks in the corridor wiped everything out. Somebody kept on opening the doors, going inside, then going back out, shutting the door and going on to the next. The locks of the doors, opening and shutting, rattled.

I went out into the corridor with my pen in my hand.

In the room opposite (where Lado's lady-friend was living) Luydmila Pavlovna stood in profile in front of the mirror in all the magnificence of her golden hair-do, splendid bust and immense hips, turning first this way then that.

The occupant of the room was absent.

"O dear, I thought you'd gone, too," said Lyudmila Pavlovna, slightly embarrassed. "There's an interesting film today. Everybody's there, only it's very grim. I didn't go, I find it too much for me . . . I've had enough troubles in my life as it is."

She came out into the corridor and locked the door behind her.

"I got quite mixed up," she explained in reply to my questioning glance. "There's a mirror here in one of the rooms which makes me look a little slimmer, not quite so well built. . . . Whilst everybody else watches a film I walk around and look . . . It's laughable, isn't it? But a woman is always a woman, even at 40. Don't you agree, Nina Sergeyevna?"

"You're not 40, more like 55," I thought. "And it's not just to look at yourself that you go into the rooms, opening them with your key when the occupants aren't at home."

All this passed through my mind now as I watched Lyudmila Pavlovna approach. "You're not getting thinner, you're putting on fat," I thought, gloating. But when she came to within ten paces of me my spite vanished. Lyudmila Pavlovna was crying. She was carrying a heavy box under one arm and wiping her eyes with the other, squeezing her little wet handkerchief into a lump . . . She probably thought she wouldn't meet anyone in the grove and had given reign to her tears. And now, she suddenly bumped into me. Snow, nothing but snow on both sides of the path . . . There was nowhere to turn off.

It was clear that the box was heavy and awkward. She was hardly able to carry it. It kept bumping against one of her fat thighs. Tears were flowing abundantly and the mascara made black furrows down her pink and white face.

"What's the matter, Lyudmila Pavlovna? Let me carry it a little . . . Well, at least I'll hold it for you a minute and you have a rest . . . Here, let's put it here on the tree-trunk . . . It won't come to any harm . . . And you sit down . . . just here . . . I'll brush it clean."

I didn't know what to do, nor what to say. I raked the snow off the broad tree-trunk, threw my muff onto it and made Lyudmila Pavlovna sit down on the muff. Then I gave her a clean handkerchief. She blew her nose, dried her tears, looked anxiously at me, at the path and the house and only then spoke. She was coming from the post-office. She spoke incoherently, in a whisper, fidgeting on her tree-stump and grasping my hands. From what she said I understood that she had a younger sister ("we've been orphans a long time and I love her like a daughter") and this sister had married very successfully ("her husband was so interesting—there aren't any more like him now . . . and he simply worshipped her—he was even jealous of the chair she sat on . . ."), but in 1937 he was arrested ("surely you heard that a lot of professors were imprisoned then, and he was an unusually cultured professor, there aren't any like him now") and he disappeared and she was sent off to a camp. Last year she returned, it's true not to Moscow, it was impossible to get permission to live in Moscow, but to Vladimir, where she got a job ("she has no profession so she went to work in a nursery") and lived reasonably well, especially since Lyudmila Pavlova regularly sent her parcels. ("You know it's impossible from Moscow, but you can from the station here"). And yesterday she had all of a sudden received an official notice from the post office and today her parcel had been returned. The note said: "addressee unknown". And some woman in the queue—she had a mother in Vladimir—had said that all the former prisoners had been re-arrested in the course of a single night and sent off somewhere to the north. ("She used a word . . . I can't quite remember it . . . One's mind goes a complete blank from all this anxiety . . . it sounded like something 'timers', 'second-timers' . . . it sounded like something 'timers', 'second-timers'—that means for the second time . . . those who have been in camp once").

Lyudmila Pavlovna was silent. The word 'second-timers' kept hammering in my mind. She sat on my muff not saying a word and covering my handkerchief with red and black smudges.

"You'll get cold here," I said, not knowing what to say. "Let's go, I'll help you to carry the box."

Second-timers. Those who have already been released once are being sent back a second time.

We started walking.

"They might also take Bilibin," I thought.

"Only carry it with the address towards you, like that," Lyudmila Pavlovna said to me. "Otherwise they'll see the address and guess at once. . . . Vladimir was the place where there were many exiles . . . They were not allowed to live in Moscow but in Vladimir it was alright. But now they are picking everybody up even from there . . . I didn't mention it in the form. Last year our director dismissed a nurse. She had concealed the fact that she had a husband who had been arrested . . . What do you think, will they start large scale arrests again? And all because of those Jews!

"What do you mean, because of the Jews?" I asked, stopping.

"Don't you read the papers?" Lyudmila Pavlovna whispered. "There's some sort of plot again. They're stirring up something. Some kind of 'cosmopolitans' have been uncovered. They hatch plots (they've all got relatives abroad), and innocent people are tortured on their account. It's not so easy to sort them out. It's bound to be like that . . . Because of those tramps and traitors honest people have to suffer. You think it's easy for the security authorities to make it all out when there are so many of them?"

I felt like flinging her box into the snow but couldn't think what to say. How could one rid her poor mind of this garbage? This was why the press and radio spewed up their insistent, stupid lies. For this was not the old, spontaneous anti-semitism nor the anti-semitism which was brought to us again from fascist Germany during the war, when one could hear in queues the words: "the Jews don't go short", "the Jews know how to get things done" and when a certain old woman from Uzbekistan said proudly to an old Jewish lady in my presence: "My Uzbek eyes don't want to see you . . ." This was no spontaneous madness which so often in our past had seized ignorant people. This time it was a madness deliberately organized, planned and spread, with a carefully thought-out purpose. I could only say, helplessly: "What on earth have the Jews got to do with it?" We walked as far as the stairs of one of the Finnish houses where the staff lived. Lyudmila Pavlovna swept up the steps and I handed her the box.

"How very kind of you!" Lyudmila Pavlovna said in a loud voice, as though dismissing an accompanying admirer.

I stood there for a while, not knowing where to go. I saw so clearly the inevitable connection. Again those lies from which blood would gush forth once more. It was as though I had touched both with my hand.

"Second-timers . . ." Again Bilibin. I recalled that I had already heard the word in Moscow. Some time last year.

It was too early to return home. I walked along the path towards the road. I imagined that no more would be asked of me that day, but the Stage-Director who had staged it all, had decided otherwise.

The gloomy stout gentleman with high blood pressure caught me up half-way down the hill and, puffing away, walked beside me. There was nothing to be done. I slowed down because he was not allowed to walk quickly. We went a little way in silence.

"What's your pressure today?" I asked mechanically.

"It's not going down," replied the stout gentleman. "It's 190 on 110. I'm on my way to meet Ekaterina Ivanovna. She promised to bring me a new medicine from Moscow."

Ekaterina Ivanovna was our doctor.

"You should probably be lying down," I said, looking at his miserably drooping moustache. We were descending the same hill as when Bilibin, the journalist and I went for a walk together for the first time. Only it was light now; the snow-clad forest seemed welcoming, kind; and for that reason that dark evening had receded far into the past. And also because I hadn't known Bilibin at all then, but now . . .

I looked at the soft white hump of the grave, at the bridge below. . . . The obelisk of the tomb was crowned with a white ball of snow.

"Have you read the papers today?" the stout gentleman asked wheezing. "Our Sergei Dimitriyevich made a whole speech . . ."

"Yes, it was disgusting," I said and held the fat man for a second by his sleeve, because he almost slipped. "Every day you eat with a person who is a man like any other man, and suddenly he starts playing the same tune as those scoundrels . . . And he told me himself, three days ago, that these critics are first-class experts on the theatre . . ."

"What can one do? . . . Wife, children . . ." the fat man said quietly with a sigh. "You know, a family man can't run any risk . . ."

He stopped, out of breath, and started to rewind his coarse ginger-coloured scarf round his neck. The only warm thing he had on. He was wearing a shabby autumn coat. He had difficulty in lifting his short arms, his face grew purple and his eyes opened wide. I wanted to help him tie his scarf again, as though he were a little boy but I didn't like to. "How will he climb up the hill if he got out of breath coming down?" I thought.

"Your wife is in Moscow?" I asked, for the sake of saying something.

"No," the fat man had managed to tie his scarf and began to hobble down again. "The Germans burnt her."

"What?" I cried out.

"Yes, burnt her. In a ghetto. In Minsk. And two children. We had three children. Two boys and a girl. Grisha, Yasha and Sonya. Now I have one son left, Yasha. He's at my aunt's whilst I'm being treated here. But usually he and I live together."

We had reached the bridge but I didn't even notice it. They'd burnt his wife and children. And what did Pushkin say? "The kindled stove is crackling . . . It's good to ponder by the stove." I brushed a large white pillow off the railings. One must grasp this clearly—logs are burnt and children are burnt. But my heart didn't want to grasp it clearly . . . The fat man was standing in the middle of the bridge, looking ahead in the direction from which he expected the doctor to come. The names of Grisha and Sonya constricted my breathing. One had to make the conversation sound ordinary to learn to breathe again.

"What part of Moscow do you live in?" I enquired, as though after your children have been burnt, the district you live in has any meaning.

"Oh, Krasnaya Presnya street."

We continued standing.

"Your boy, Yasha, goes to school?" I asked ineptly.

82

Each word of mine seemed false. What can one talk about, what can one ask a father, a husband, when his wife and children have been burnt? Of course I knew already that the Germans burnt Jews, but it was the first time that I had seen a man who had gone through this. The fat man kept answering in his naïve and trusting way. He told me what marks his only son, who had not been burnt, got at school and how Yasha himself made his own bed in the morning and made tea.

"Is it a . . . good school, then?" I asked, afraid lest he should stop talking and I would have to think of Grisha and Sonya again.

"It's a good school," the fat man replied. "It has a gymnasium and hot lunches. Only . . . how shall I put it . . . international education is badly done . . . My Yasha pronounces his 'r's' badly and the other children tease him."

He very humbly used the words: 'other children', and not 'nasty boys' and instead of using the word 'anti-semitism' he said: 'the international education is badly done.' He wasn't panting more than usual and his round eyes weren't noticeably wider than they were normally. I felt I had had enough of questions, of necks shot through, dogs, stoves and second-timers. When I saw in the distance our doctor's knitted hat I decided that I could leave the patient in her care. I said good-bye, "Until lunch!" and walked towards the house.

I wanted to get to my room as quickly as possible—no, not to my room, but to room No. 8. I wanted to tell him everything, about the newspapers, Lyudmila Pavlovna, the box, about the fat gentleman—and, if I had the strength, about the children. But when I went into Bilibin's room with tears in my throat the science fiction writer and Valentina Nikolayevna were sitting there. The science fictionist was explaining about the roots of Zionism in our country which it was essential to extirpate. Bilibin didn't argue, but began to explain that the people of the future would be feeding on special nutritious tablets and not eating soup and cutlets, vegetables and bread. "You would just swallow a tablet and would feel no hunger for the rest of the day."

"How horrible! Some sort of pills! And supposing I should want some nice cake?" Valentina Nikolayevna asked flirtatiously.

"You've only to say cakes and they will be at your feet, or rather, at your lips," Bilibin gallantly replied.

I only stayed for five minutes and then hurried to my room.

After supper I went out for a walk and descended the dark road to the stream alone. Again the dark forest had closed in on the road, again, as it had been then, it was difficult to make out the grave beneath the branches of the firs. The ravine was flooded with moonlight. I stood for a while on the bridge, listening to the rhythm of the power station. What did it produce there? Was it only electric current? Could it not perhaps be time? It would tap out another thirteen days—and that would be the end of my stay here. And then Moscow.

Against the thumping of the power station I strained my ears to catch the sound of the stream. On that first evening with Bilibin he had said: "sometimes it comes, sometimes it disappears." I caught the sound of the pure childish babble of the water. "Dear chatter-brook," I thought and walked home. Now I would go to bed. With this word, perhaps it might be easier to fall asleep.

. . . And the fat man was worrying about his high blood-pressure! Was looking for a new medicine. Was wanting to get well! Wanting to live, live, live, bearing within him the memory of the children who had been burnt, like logs. But by what means did he destroy his memory in order to fall asleep? And by what means did I? For I lived with the memory of Alyosha's last smile and slept and even last night had slept after learning about the back of the neck. And Bilibin lived with the memory of how he had tied the tag on the leg of his dear friend, Sasha. And knowing that any moment he might end up there a second time—become a 'second-timer'—the first time for no reason at all and the second time because he had been there the first time.

The fat man still had a son left. I had Katya. One had to live.

No, not just for Katya. But for future friends—brothers, to whom I would be able to tell everything.

. . . March 1949

Early in the morning, instead of working, I sat down to write letters. Lyudmila Pavlovna was going to town that evening and had promised to post them. "Well, I've got to look round the shops for various things . . ." Lyudmila Pavlovna explained in the dining-room, but I gathered that she wanted to try to find out in Moscow about her sister.

So I sat down to write letters. I wrote to Katya and tried to give each word the tenderness I felt at the mere mention of her name and to make each word a talisman for her, a kind of safe conduct. To protect her from misfortune and disasters. During the war she had been small and it had been easier to protect her. Then she had only been physically defenceless; she had not been frightened by vulgarity, coarseness and denunciation; it had been possible to hide her from bombs in the underground, in a ship's hold or cattle truck. Press her close to me, rock her, wrap her up, take her away. When she had been with me she had not been afraid of anything. Holding my hand, she had not feared the black spot in the sky between two white swords, the roar of the anti-aircraft guns in our dacha garden, the early morning rattle of shrapnel against the trunks of the pine-trees. She was with her mother. What could be more reassuring? But now, even if I was near at hand, how could I protect her soul from being wounded?

I felt I wanted to write not a letter to Katya but a prayer for her to someone all-powerful.

> Not for my own barren soul do I pray,
> The soul of the pilgrim, with no home in the
>   world,
> But I want to entrust an innocent maid
> To the warmth of Our Lady from the cold
>   of the world.*

How could Lermontov—a mere youth, an hussar—nurture in his soul this prayer, full of the tenderness of motherhood? But, in any case, everything about him was a mystery.

I also tried to write to my friends but here I had no success. "Life's fine". But what about news from that other world? And Lyolka? "I walk a great deal." Could one call strolling here really going for walks? Was it not rather "an attempt to fish something out of the pit of what one had lived through"? But what you fished out you wouldn't entrust to the post.

"Well, how's your translation going? I'm very worried about your meeting with the editor," I wrote to Tanya Polykova and asked her a host of questions just to avoid writing about myself. How could we write proper letters!

When we met I could tell her everything. At one time Tanya and I shared the same desk at school. She understood everything. She remembered Alyosha and I could talk about everything to her. Apart from her I had no "understanders" left. Katya was still too small. (And suppose all of a sudden she were to grow up and not understand either? School would teach her not to understand, the newspapers would teach her not to understand.)

Suddenly I heard the shuffling of slippers and a small cough near my door. There was silence for a second, then came a knock.

"Come in!"

I knew that Bilibin was not getting up yet, that it could not be him, and yet I felt really sorry when I saw Veksler instead.

Under his arm he had a file with torn pieces of tape. He looked embarrassed and gloomy.

"You promised to listen to my poems," he said, looking at the floor. "But I haven't seen you anywhere . . . Oh! you were writing . . . I've interrupted you . . . I don't think one is supposed to visit one another here, but you've been going to see Bilibin . . . And so I've come to see you."

"Bilibin is ill, but I'm not," I might have said, but I felt sorry for him and didn't say anything. I pushed the letter away from me with pleasure.

"I'll listen! Do please sit down and read them to me."

Casting a sidelong glance at my letter, which put him off because it reminded him that he had come at an inopportune moment, he opened the file and took out the poems. There were the originals, word for word translations, and ordinary translations. He kept looking for something, chiding himself and making excuses.

Finally he began. First he would read the poem in Yiddish, then retell it to me in Russian, then I would take it up and read through the translation aloud myself.

The poems riveted one's attention. There was much in them which reflected his premature grey hair, his youthfulness, his nervous hands. They were serious, sad poems about the war.

Nothing makes it so apparent than the helplessness of a translation that verse is created not merely, indeed, not so much from words, thoughts, metres, and images, but from the weather, nervousness, from silence, separation . . . Not only from the black lines of print, but also from the gaps between the lines, deep pauses which govern the breathing—and the soul . . . How can one translate the gap between the lines, the air gathered up by the lungs between two quatrains?

There's a rustle and crunch: it feels good here;
A flaming white bush of roses—
Every morning the frost's more severe—
Bows its dazzling ice-crusted head.

And on the rich snows in full dress
There are ski-tracks—a mere memory
Of long ages ago, when the two of us,
Just the two of us, rode here together.*

Here every line is clad in the icy-silver of hoar frost. But 'the wine of delight' is the white paper between the line completing the first quatrain and the first line of the second. To look at, the gap is just a gap, but it is just here that one draws into one's lungs the frosty air in a kind of exhaustion from the anticipation of grief and happiness—and perhaps from climbing the hill:

And on the rich snows in full dress
There are ski-tracks—a mere memory

The voice sinks on the word 'memory' because the heart sinks when remembering. A track in one's soul and a track on the rich snows.

Poetry is surely just that mysterious something which remains untranslatable after the most careful, the most musical translation. One can translate words and rhythms but how does one translate a track in the snow that so happily wounds the memory?

Of course I didn't attempt to convey these obscure thoughts to the person listening to me. He kept sitting down, jumping up, and rubbing his small, frost-bitten, blue hands. I read the translations aloud, and without mentioning their complete inadequacy, pointed out which line was rather more natural, more harmonious and which more awkward. That was all. But even this uncomplicated operation impressed my companion.

"How well you understand poetry," he said again, sinking into an arm chair, as though tired. "Do you really not write yourself?"

"I've already told you that I don't."

I conscientiously read out all the translations down to the last, I made one or two corrections as I went along and proposed to ask the translator about some points.

He jumped up and began putting his papers in the file and thanking me over-profusely. He tried to tie a knot with some pieces of tape but they were too short. And the sheets of paper were sticking out.

I suddenly felt that I wanted him to go away as soon as possible. Because I understood—how does one understand such things?—that he didn't want to go away from me and that I had come to occupy a big place in his life—it was none of my wanting, and, perhaps, against his own wishes; that my room for him was the same as No. 8 for me. And that parting from it he felt the pain of separation . . . he couldn't even manage to tie up the tapes.

"Will you go for a walk today, after tea?" he asked, finally leaving the tapes alone.

"I don't know yet . . . it depends on the situation: my heart, the weather, work, baths . . ."

He wanted to say something, but merely moved his lips, said nothing and went out.

And so I didn't succeed in writing any letters in time for Lyudmila Pavlovna's departure—only the one letter to Katya. Immediately after Neksler left the girl—Lyolka's cousin who worked 'in the store'—came to change the bed-linen.

Whilst I was reading with no particular interest, I kept watching her. I noticed that when she hung clean towels over the back of the bed she stood on tiptoe and from a distance cast a sidelong glance at the book lying on my table. It was *Hatter's Castle.*

"Have you read the book?" I asked.

"No, where would I get it from!" she said, pulling the clean pillow slip onto the pillow.

"But do you usually read a lot? Or have you no time?"

"Where would one find the time or the books?"

"There's a large library here," I said.

"Large library!" she repeated suddenly and with such sarcasm and long accumulated venom that I felt uncomfortable: "It's no good asking the librarian; she says it's not for the villagers."

"Would you like to go to Moscow one day? To study? They might give you a place in a hostel."

"That's what you think!" She answered contemptuously "Not for the likes of us. The Germans were here for eighteen months so we're from occupied territory. They won't even give us permission to live in town . . .

And you talk about a place in a hostel!"

She seized the dirty linen in her arms and went towards the door.

"How old are you now? Seventeen? Nineteen? So when the Germans were here you were eight! Not more! As old as Lyolka is now!" I shouted. "How can that have any importance now?"

She didn't deign to answer. "Where on earth have you been all this time, you old fool?" was what her back seemed to say. "Sitting here, writing. And what they write they don't even know themselves."

And it was true—I was an old fool! If she had been not eight, but seventeen or twenty-five or thirty under the Germans what difference would that have made? How could she be blamed if the army when it retreated had thrown them on the mercy of the enemy—and what an enemy! It was Hitler, not Napoleon. They were left behind and now they had to pay for it! It was quite alright under Napoleon to surrender half Russia and then reconquer it; ordinary people had suffered no harm. But in this case when they retreated they had left Lyolka's mother and Lyolka behind as well; they had left them not just to anybody but to murderers. The forest and the fields could be reconquered, but what about the people? How many such Lyolkas and their mothers had been missing after victory!

The murderers had been driven out. But Lyolka was branded: "I was in the occupation." And she and her mother and cousin were no longer fully-fledged citizens. . . You couldn't escape filling out forms: these forms were like a barrier placed in front of their lives.

. . . After lunch I paid a short visit to Bilibin. He was no longer in bed, but was sitting in an arm chair at the table behind a typewriter. He was glad to see me and bade me sit down, but I could see that he wanted to work, so I thought I'd better go back to my room—after all I hadn't yet done a stroke of work all day. "Supposing I were to show him . . . the manuscript . . . where I go under," the vague thought occurred to me. Was it possible that only one person—Tanya Polykova—would read it in my life time? Perhaps there were indeed, many more 'understanders' than I and Tanya thought. He should understand if anyone could! He was one of us.

"I'm finishing," he said, triumphantly. "I'm writing the last chapter. I shall soon be sealing up the envelope and sending it off to the publishers."

And an expression of anxiety slid over his face—over that calm, hawk-like face.

"I have a favour to ask of you. Will you read my manuscript, when I've finished it? Veksler said you have an amazing understanding of literature . . ."

"Of course, I'll read it. It will be a joy for me," I said. I wanted to add: "It will be again like it was in the forest: I shall hear your real voice."But I restrained myself.

. . . March 1949

This morning after breakfast I completed with ease the quota of my translation. I took a bath, lay down in the bright room, reflecting the glare of the snow, and read *Hatter's Castle* for a while, then took a turn to the main road and back; I admired the hazel grove in the gully, fancifully decked out with hoar-frost, and feeling hungry, bright and for some reason not unhappy, went downstairs to my table. Bilibin was already sitting there with a napkin tucked under his collar and engaged in an animated conversation with Sergei Dimitrievich who had only just got back from Moscow. Somebody else was sitting at our table. It was Pyotr Ivanovich Klokov, the literary critic in charge of book reviews on one of the Moscow journals. No sooner had I been introduced to him than my *joie de vivre* vanished. He was a puny figure with a dull, shiny, lumpy face, wearing fashionable patent-leather shoes and a bow-tie. I took an immediate dislike to him. He looked like some sort of foppish boor. I disliked the way he greeted me with his exaggerated mannerisms and the way he told off the waitress, Liza, because the soup was not hot enough, the way he gave a little hitch to his trousers to keep the crease in place and the way he said "Here's to your health" every time he emptied his glass. Over soup, he and Sergei Dimitrievich started to recount the literary news from Moscow.

The conversation resolved around the *Literary Gazette* the *Soviet Writer*, the committees of the Writer's Union and the editorial offices of the reviews.

Bilibin said nothing, he was either silent or asked questions and listened very attentively to his companions, glancing at me from time to time from beneath half-closed eyelids. Klokov entertained us by announcing that he was now working on problems of craftsmanship, not on old material but on new. He was studying the style of the works of Bubbenov, Perventsev and Orest Maltsev.* Sergei Dimitrievich mildly remarked that, although he considered the general slant of the article to be absolutely correct, yet one had to acknowledge that the style of these writers lagged somewhat behind the content. Then Sergei Dimitrievich talked about the speech of the chief editor at the *Literary Gazette* meeting.

"It's extraordinary how he was able to show up the

grain of imperialist seed in the worthless cosmopolitan ideas. How he managed to expose them. Amazing! His speech opened my eyes to a lot of things. For example . . . Zelenin, a good friend of mine . . ."

"Oh, isn't his real name . . . Zelikson?" Klokov interrupted with a grin.

"Yes. Zelenin. A friend of mine; we were in the army together and he's a neighbour of mine in the country. I have often accepted his articles in our journal. . . . Of course, not because he was a friend, but simply because, as you know, he has a doctor's degree and the reputation of an expert . . ."

"Yes, they all manage to do that—boast of their erudition," Klokov put in.

"I published him without noticing, without wishing to notice what lay behind his love for Flaubert, Stendhal . . . it was only after the speech of the chief editor that I clearly saw which way he was gravitating. I recalled a conversation we once had when playing cards. He said: "I suppose without the French there wouldn't have been the psychologism of Tolstoy.""

With a serious and meaningful look Sergei Dimitrievich glanced round the table.

"Just imagine. According to him it wasn't our Tolstoy's influence on the whole world, but the French who influenced Tolstoy!"

"Yes, they certainly knew how to push their own ideas," said the critic and took out a gold cigarette-case. "Do you mind?" he asked, turning to me. He snapped the case shut and lit a cigarette. "Pushing cheap anti-Soviet ideas. And they certainly knew how to look after one another. My assistant in our review had a lot of them in tow . . . They were queueing up . . . Now he's been dismissed and ticked off. As if you're likely to cure them merely by a ticking-off. You can rest assured, there's a whole trade-union of them."

"What was his name?" Bilibin wanted to know for some reason or other.

"Landau: I went on leave and he published Meerovich.* And Meerovich used to praise . . . what was his name? Mikhoels,* do you remember? He published him and I nearly got a severe reprimand . . . And I have to admit, I was careless in not noticing it . . . until the press came out with an explanation."

"And what . . . to be precise . . . did the press explain to you?" I asked. My heart had been hammering away in my throat, in my ears for a long time. So strong was its beat that for seconds it drowned the voice of the person speaking.

"Everything," Klokov gave a slight shrug of his shoulders. "Their anti-Soviet activity and anti-Soviet bias. Links with America. How deeply Zionism has taken root."

"What strikes me when I read the papers," I said quietly and with an effort, "is that everything they write about these people is, on the contrary, blatantly untrue. It's the blatancy of the lies that strikes one, that is so palpably obvious." I wanted to add: "and the similarity that the words bear to those of 1937—" but Providence saved me and I restrained myself. "They're not real words but a sort of empty shell. Dummies. You know when you give a baby a dummy? Without any milk . . . It's the same with the words. They lack content, there's nothing inside them. They're just shorthand symbols, not sentences."

Bilibin kicked me under the table with his foot. But I could no longer stop myself. It was just as well that I hadn't named the year.

"Not a single word that has real value. Therefore it's quite clear that neither Zelenin nor his friends are guilty in any way."

"The blatancy of the lies?" queried Sergei Dimitrievich, "Dummies?"

"Nina Sergevena, you mustn't, you really mustn't be soft-hearted and stand up for all and sundry," said Klokov for my edification. "To show magnanimity . . . when international reaction is increasingly active, is extremely dangerous, extremely dangerous."

How many times had I heard that objection in 1937! How can you vouch for everybody? How can you know them so well? Of course, I didn't, for the 'enemies' were counted in their millions. How could I vouch for everyone? But I could vouch for the firm turning out the lies. I would always be able to make out its trademark. The conveyor-belt of the patented lie—how many times in my lifetime it had started up! How could I fail to recognize it?

At that moment the gleaming cuff-links of Klokov with their large stones seemed particularly detestable. When he poked the bread with his fork they shone.

"You can't possibly know everybody and vouch for everybody," Klokov repeated, revealing his steel-capped teeth in a condescending smile. "You can't vouch for everybody. Don't you agree?"

"I don't know. I have never even seen one of the accused with my own eyes, let alone all of them," I said. "But there's not one grain of truth in what they write about them. That I can vouch for . . . One can hear it immediately . . . They're not thoughts, but ready-made clichés. One can hear it in the monotony . . . in the word order . . . in the syntax . . . tone . . . intonation."

Klokov would have laughed in my face, if someone

authoritarian had not recently explained to him that under all circumstances one must remain polite in the company of ladies, especially at table and especially if they are complete idiots.

Sergei Dimitrievich gazed at me with compassion and surprise. Just imagine! One has to distinguish truth from falsehood by the tone of the words, not by the sense, but by their tone and arrangement! What nonsense! What gibberish she talks, and she's a translator, a member of the Union . . . It's not surprising she loves the poetry of . . . that . . . obscure . . . Pasternak.

"If words won't convince you," said Klokov, "then there are some facts for you which confirm the un-patriotic activity of certain non-Russian nationalistic groups . . . groupings . . . cliques . . . linked, so to speak, with cosmopolitan critics by an ideological—and not only ideological—relationship. The day before yesterday the publishing-house Emes was closed down and those in charge arrested. What further proof do you want?"

I caught the sound of a chair being moved back and glanced round, Veksler came up to our table.

"Emes has been closed down?"

"Yes, Emes," Klokov snapped with satisfaction.

"That's just what I said, Emes."

He stopped eating and adjusted his tie looking very pleased with himself.

Veksler stood in silence in front of our table.

"And those in charge have been arrested," Klokov repeated.

"Well, friends, isn't it time we went to our rooms?" Bilibin said in a loud voice.

Everyone got up.

I had finished, finished! Finished my writing! I didn't know yet what it would be called, perhaps—'Lamp on the Bridge' or perhaps simply 'Daughter'. Here it lay in front of me, written, rewritten, finished. I turned over the pages and corrected the pagination. I would stick it into my diary. A single note-book was easier to hide than two.

I knew nothing about it, what it was like. If only someone would read it and tell me.

The stars shone faintly in the sky far away. The snow did not crunch beneath my feet but lay in silence, perhaps so as not to remind me of a happy Christmas Eve in my childhood. All the lights on the bridge went out simultaneously and like everything that night the suddenness and soundlessness of their disappearance seemed to me frightening. I had taken up my place in the queue the evening before—number 715. They would start letting us in from nine o'clock. It couldn't be six yet as no trains could be heard. Women were wandering silently along the embankment next to the frozen parapet. It seemed as though the frost had implanted all its strength in the ringing granite wall—if you touched it you would burn yourself. The last of the night lingered on, but no one had hopes for the morning, although the dark was growing paler every minute and the white of scarves on shoulders and the outline of roofs and chimneys on the houses stood out in relief. Women were emerging from dirty doorways, unsteady on their feet. They had dozed on first and second-floor landings, on the frozen stone slabs. But now the first green spark flashed above the pale bulk of the bridge and from there came the rattle of a tram—it was morning for sure—and greenish faces and piles of dirty snow flung out, onto the ice, appeared in the thin blend of light. In the windows of houses lights were already visible.

As soon as the trams started up the numbers of people increased. As they approached the door where they had been told to wait, the newcomers would pull out of their pockets, handbags and mittens, their numbers on a crumpled piece of paper and would proffer them to the self-appointed keeper of the list and immediately a bad-tempered row would flare up: "We've been freezing here the whole night!", somebody said, "and you booked your place and went off to warm yourself. And here we are queueing up for you! Cross the lot off and that'll be that!"—and in those bad-tempered words I thought I heard the sound that I caught in the lonely universal silence of that night: each woman was thinking that it was her Petya who had been wrongfully taken and the husband of this woman and of this one and this one was a traitor to his country, a saboteur, a spy . . . One should keep as far away, as far away from them as possible.

It had grown quite light. And I saw how many women there were with infants. The babies were coughing and sneezing in their mother's arms, their faces hidden under white shawls. They were wriggling and grunting in the warmth of thick blankets and the mothers, thrusting their hands into the warmth, would anxiously feel their infants, rock and squeeze the living bundles to themselves and go off into the entrances of the buildings to feed them.

By eight o'clock everyone had made their way from the embankment onto the street and, timidly huddling against the wall and trying to take up as little space as possible, formed a queue facing the tall, official-looking door of the Big House. The door was such a long way off that I could only just make out its outlines. An old Jewess, the hair of her upper lip covered in hoar-frost, was standing in front of me, clad in two thick shawls—one grey, the other white—and behind me a young blond woman stood with an infant in her arms. Somehow the baby had been wrapped up unusually skilfully, snugly and elegantly. There was a little pink, knitted, blanket and over its tiny face starched, bluish tulle. A broad velvet ribbon held its tiny feet together and the mother wore a knitted hat and knitted mittens to match—clearly she had made everything herself.

"Is it a boy?" I asked.

"A girl," she replied and from her accent I guessed at once that she was a Finn. "Afraid got cold, she sick . . . She four months."

The little baby girl sneezed beneath the starched pale-blue cloud, her mother lifted the tulle and I caught a glimpse of a tiny delicate face, pink like her blanket, so delicate that a speck of ash, which had settled on her cheek looked like a heavy, black, stone. She was blessed with eyelashes which seemed to reach halfway down her cheeks. She had a teeny little face—and there in the blanket were tiny red heels, tiny little fingers with tiny toy nails and all her fragrant velvety little body.

"Wrap her up quickly," I said. It was terrible to think that the frost might touch that little face. "Is it long since your husband was arrested?"

"Two weeks. Lorry came to our village at night and carry off all men. We Finns . . ."

They hadn't opened the doors yet, but the morning was already aflame, making the snow sparkle with a frosty brilliance, and the street was beginning to throng with people. Neat little school-girls in twos and threes were striding in a businesslike way over the untouched snow of the road. With pig-tails which their mothers had tightly plaited and in their stout little felt boots they whispered together and laughed, whilst the boys slid over bare, icy patches, and stared around about them. One of them threw off his satchel, went up to a bench and carefully lay down on the heap of snow. He lay down —and at once felt bored. He jumped up and, shaking himself, examined for some time his imprint, pressed out in the snow. Little children craned their necks, halted and peered at our frozen faces and then ran, stumbling, to catch each other up . . . Grown-ups were already hurrying to work. Scarcely anyone of the grown-ups looked at us or asked about anything, perhaps because they knew already who we were, or because a person, hurrying to a government office, had no curiosity in any case. Only some woman with a basket and wearing glasses tied together with string suddenly asked as she passed:

"What's this queue for, comrades?"

Nobody answered her. Everyone was looking at the wall or at the ground.

"What are you standing there for?" the inquisitive woman repeated.

"Are you envious?" somebody from the queue suddenly snarled. "Join the queue, 'who's the last—I'm behind you' " . . .

The woman went away. Her question had made me suffer more acutely than the whole cheerless, frosty night. I felt mute. I could not have given her an answer. This night and all the preceding nights and days I had been tormented not by grief but by something worse: the incomprehensibility and namelessness of what was taking place. Grief? Was grief really like that? Grief has a name and if you have sufficient courage you find the strength to pronounce it. But what had happened to us had no name because it made no sense. A dream, a nightmare? No, one has no right to cast such a slur on nightmares. My head seemed to be spinning and my heart gradually growing heavier not from the sixteen hours spent on my feet but from fruitless efforts to grasp what had happened and give it a name. My thoughts would reach a certain point—I think it was the moment when alien hands rummaged amongst the children's toys looking for guns—and would keep dwelling on those hands and the children's bricks (which formed a picture of a little fairy-tale hut or, if the bricks were turned over all together, of a large white goat); or my thoughts would fix themselves on that goat and refuse to go any further. I could no more go any further than waggle my ears. I would purse my lips and frown, but all to no avail. What movement could I make, flex which muscle?

At last the queue of people in front of me started to move; the heavy doors had opened. The queue, quietly and apprehensively, poured into a huge multi-windowed hall. There was no pushing, no noise, no bickering— merely frightened looks. For it was not the staircase where people spat or the corridor of the public prosecutor's office, nor the little crooked, wooden rooms facing the information window of the prison but the Big House itself, the Commissariat, fate itself. Even before entering the hall women would hastily shake the snow from their shawls and felt boots and, having crossed the threshold, gaze fearfully at the massive wooden blocks of the floor, as though a trap-door lay concealed beneath. Afraid to lean against the severe, noble, stately columns, they quietly shifted from one foot to the other, asking each other their numbers and ranging themselves along the walls and they screwed up their eyes to look at the high, straight, spotlessly clean windows, which gazed into the broad light of day.

Immediately, the commandant appeared in the hall. He didn't enter but appeared as though from underneath a stage-floor. He was made up as a gaoler, with all the tasteless effrontery of a provincial opera. Heavy keys were jangling at his waist. His revolver-holster was undone. The trunk of his body was long, but his legs short, as though they were not his own, but borrowed from someone else. And over his face, bloated and lacking sleep, above the dirty-yellow pallor of his forehead was the bright blue band of his cap. As soon as he had appeared he started rearranging the queue which had been standing in perfect order anyhow. He kept ordering the women about as though he was dealing with horses, shoving them by the shoulders and banging his thighs with his keys.

"Hey, you girls! Make the line straighter! One behind another! Mothers to the right! Who do you think I'm talking to? Women with children form a separate queue! Make way for mothers and children! One place in every five will be taken by a mother! Five girls—one mother! Four of you will go in and then there will be a mother. Got it? You'll go in when you hear the bell . . . And where the devil has such a crowd of you come from today?"

Some lowered their eyes and turned away, trying not to look at him, others, with a pitifully feigned jauntiness, smiled and took the liberty of asking questions:

"Please, comrade commandant, they'll give us some information here, won't they . . . why he was arrested . . . what I mean is, what's he accused of, what the charge is?"

"Please tell me, comrade commandant, if they'll accept my statement . . . my husband's in the third stage . . . of tuberculosis . . ."

"Of course I do apologise, most frightfully," said the old Jewess with the moustache, "but when they·send my husband off we shall be granted a meeting, no?"

The commandant who was standing kind of sideways on to the women questioning him and banging his thighs with the keys, broke the silence of the whole huge hall in a stentorian voice:

"Why the devil do you come here in any case? You merely upset yourselves and interrupt the work of the staff. Since your husbands have been taken there must be something in the accusation. What else is there to ask? They don't take an honest man without some reason . . . You girls should look out for some other man for yourselves instead of coming here to no purpose." He winked. "You're young and attractive."

I expected him at any moment to overdo it and pinch one of them under the chin.

The young woman with the child had become separated from me. She was standing much closer to the door than I, in the special queue for women and children.

The interviewing started. Every two or three minutes there would be a short, distinct, sharp ring and someone, pressing her passport to her breast like an ikon, would disappear through the door. All those standing in the queue would have liked very much to see the one who had already had her interview, to rush over to her, overcoming their repulsion for her as the wife of a spy, in order to find out what she'd been told, but not one of them returned to the hall. Evidently there was a special exit onto the street from the room where the information was handed out . . . And fresh women kept arriving. It became more and more stuffy in the hall and a watery heaviness was setting into my legs. The bright light of the windows hurt my eyes.

The bell rang every three minutes and every three minutes the next woman would at once cross the threshold as though this sudden sound had been directly connected to her heart. . . . The young woman with the child was now very close. My attention was caught by the way she held her little girl, somehow oddly, on arms stretched out straight, and kept watching the tall door without blinking. But I did not worry about her and the child because I was already close to the door myself and the moment had arrived to give a last thought to the words which I would soon have to say.

The whole night long I had put off thinking what I would say on the morrow to the man giving out information, what I would ask him and, most important of all, how I would explain everything to him—I had put it off until the moment when I would at last get into the warmth. But now the stuffiness was proving too much for me. It could not be put off any longer. I had to prepare the exact words so as not to lose them at the critical moment. I had to learn them by heart because I knew by experience that as soon as I saw the face and eyes of the man sitting at the big table, running through the cards with the names of those arrested, I would be overwhelmed by the feeling of the uselessness of each word. It had already happened often enough. And I would go away again without having asked about the main thing and without having said half of what I felt must be said. Other women would implore, swear, insist, weep, their hands clutched to their breasts. And if I were to prepare myself thoroughly and think of all the right words beforehand, perhaps, I could break through the reluctance of the man to listen to me and he would make a note in his book or on the card with the name . . .

Trying not to see or hear what was going on around I began to prepare for the coming meeting. The first point was medical research work (I had put in my passport reports on Alyosha's research work written by the greatest authorities in that field). The second was teaching, the third, practical work. . . For some reason I couldn't recall anything convincing which would make everyone understand immediately what sort of person it concerned. And the bell kept ringing more and more often, the young woman with the baby had already disappeared through the door; now it was the turn of the lady in furs who had wanted to speak to me on the embankment that night, but had been afraid; and after me came the old Jewish woman, sighing loudly and, without thinking where she was, mumbling something aloud in Yiddish. . . . But my turn came first and I hadn't managed to prepare what I wanted to say . . . The next bell would be for me. I was already standing right by the door. I could touch its brown, polished surface with my hand.

The bell rang. I pushed the heavy handle and the door opened, yielding unexpectedly easily. The other side there was no hall, no reception room with portraits and a large table which I had expected when I gazed at the bronze handle, but some kind of cubby-hole, And there was no-one, nothing there—neither chair nor man. Only a warped plywood door with the inscription "Exit Here", and a closed little window—such as one finds in a post-office—in the wall on the left-hand side. I went up to the window. It was high up. To reach it I stood on tiptoe. I knocked. A shutter of plywood flew up. Framed in the window was a bald head—a tender pink colour like the fat of ham—pink, flabby cheeks and fluffy, snow-white moustache which stuck out from the soft pink flesh.

"I would like to find out," I began, standing on tiptoe.

"Who are you enquiring about?" shouted the pink head. "First name, patronymic, surname?"

I gave them.

"Who are you? Wife, sister?"

"I'm his wife."

"Papers!"

I pushed the passport into the window, dropping the references onto the floor. There was a sudden bang and the head disappeared. There was neither the moustache in front of me, nor the bald head—merely the smooth plywood board. I looked at it and tried to remember the words which I ought to say.

The plywood shutter went up. The passport came flying straight into my face.

"The case of your husband, Pimenov, Aleksei Vladimirovich, is being looked into," shouted the head. The plywood shutter again descended with a crash and I heard the bell ring in the hall.

"Exit Here" was written on the door. Since this was the exit I opened it and went out. I found myself in a little, snow-covered courtyard with sandy paths. What a release it was to breathe in the pure, frosty cold. And to see the fir-trees and the snow on the branches. I walked along, clutching passport and papers in my hand, and I felt so weak that black spots swam before my eyes. I felt I had never seen such well cleared paths, such bright yellow sand. It was a beautiful, almost cosy courtyard. I took a handful of snow and crammed it into my mouth. I came out onto the avenue. The piles of snow had already been swept from the benches, and nannies were sitting on them. The children stood near the seats like little penguins, their coat collars turned up to their very eyes—and over the collars scarves! They wore galoshes over their felt boots and stood panting in their thick coats, motionless with arms spread wide, unable to turn their necks.

The black spots overwhelmed me and I sank down onto an empty bench.

"Vell, did he give you some information, eh?" the elderly Jewess asked me in a loud whisper, as she sat down next to me and grasped me by the sleeve. Her wrinkled face, as it came closer, prevented me from seeing the snow, the children and the nannies.

"My husband's case is being looked into," I replied.

"So's mine," said the old woman. "What on earth do they want to pin on him? What is there to look into? Do they want to make spies of us? My man was a bolshevik as pure as crystal . . ."

And a crystal-pure tear slid down a deep furrow in her face. She got up and hobbled over to the tram stop. I felt that at any moment I would burst into tears, too—from the pain in my feet, from the bright snow, from the sweet penguins, who despite their scarves somehow contrived to bend over and dig in the snow. I looked around and, suddenly, through the beads of tears, I caught sight of the Finnish girl on the next bench, with her baby. It didn't occur to me immediately that it was odd that the little girl was not lying on her mother's lap but next to her on the bare frozen bench.

"Vat did he say to you, eh?" the old woman shouted to her, as she hobbled by. "Is his case being looked into?"

The girl did not answer her and the old woman, after waiting a moment, walked on. But I got up and ran over to the young mother. She was gazing somewhere beyond me and, try as I might, I couldn't fathom her look. A green, furry mitten was lying in the snow near the bench.

"I had to knock on the wooden window a second time after he'd slammed it to," I said to her, picking up the mitten. "Knock very hard to make him open it and listen to me . . . Did he slam the window in your face too? Did you manage to say anything to him?" I asked and handed the mitten to the young girl. But she didn't take it. "Why have you put the baby on the bench? There's such a frost!"

"The case being looked into," said the Finnish girl, and she still did not look at me or take the mitten from me.

I sat down beside her and carefully laid the little girl on my lap. At least she would be warmer on my lap than on the bench. The girl did not even turn her head. I pressed the pink bundle to my body. The little girl did not cry, nor did she arch her back in the blanket. I wanted to thrust my hand into the blanket, touch her little feet, but I was afraid to let the frost in.

"Is it long since you fed her?" I asked. "It's time you went home. It's time you fed her. Where do you live?"

She remained silent.

"He not have to eat any more," she said.

I gently threw off the starched coverlet.

A little dead face with a pitiful little mouth half open and with the slight gleam of an eye from under one lid was lying on my lap.

"He die already in there," said the girl. "There." And waved her arm in the direction of the building from which we had come. "But I not want to lose my place in the queue of mothers, I want get information. I much loved my husband."

We got up and hurriedly made our way to the tram stop, as though we still had somewhere to hurry to. "Loved", I thought, "loved in the past tense." I carried the heavy, dead child in my arms. "Tram No. 9", the woman said to me briefly.

"Give me!" she took the little girl from my arms and got on the tram.

. . . March 1949

How many days was it now since I hadn't kept my diary? Three? Five? I couldn't remember. I didn't know and didn't want to know. I tried to avoid knowing what today's date was. The days were already rolling down hill—towards my departure, the end, and I didn't want to count them.

Every day Bilibin and I spent many hours together, in the grove on the main road, in the fir forest, in my room, in his room. I kept thinking, perhaps I should read 'Street Lamps' to him . . . We had already told one another about our childhood and teenage years. His past was quite different from mine. He was, after all, some ten years older than I. In 1917 he had been at least twenty. His father had been a general; he broke with his father when still a boy, ran away from home, "Went off to the Revolution", as one used to say; for a short time he was a law student, got in with the S.R.'s,* fought in the Civil War—against the Whites,* against Denikin*— at first with a partisan group then in the Red Army. His whole way of life, his whole background was different from mine. But our childhood years were strangely similar in their loneliness: both my mother and his mother died young and we both grew up away from home.

In 1935 he started to write and was published; in 1937 he was arrested.

Alyosha had been arrested in August, he was arrested in the spring, in May.

Over the last few days my life here had changed. Apart from five pages of translation I did absolutely nothing. I wrote no letters, I read no books. If I was not with him I would wait for the moment when we could be together, when my treatment and his writing were finished. We would go off together for long periods and long distances—he felt well and was strong enough to walk—and people who saw us would let us go by in silence, neither addressing him, nor me, although Bilibin would playfully wave his hat and energetically shout.

"Off for a walk? Are you warmly enough dressed? Button yourself up—it's freezing!"

The grove no longer lived for itself, its own secret life, at one with the snow, wind and clouds, but existed for us, existed to imprint our footsteps in the snow, existed to cover them over in a flurry of flakes; to fill them with water, for the wind to roll over our heads; to change the colour of his eyes by the greyness or blueness of the sky; to preserve us from the whole world and not to hinder us as we listened to one another.

I could no longer read or write or be alone either under the sky, the stars or the trees. If the sunrise beyond the forest was beautiful my heart would contract; how could I convey it to him? What word should I use? If the snow on the little bridge crunched gaily under my shoes, how could I bring this sound from childhood, the sound of Christmas Eve in the country, to his room? But poetry— poetry kept us apart. We did not share poetry. He didn't understand it and didn't like it. He told me, "When I was a young boy of sixteen I wrote poetry, too." That meant it was merely a joke, a toy for him. But I kept hoping that I would remember somebody's poem that would touch him.

At my request, Nikolai Aleksandrovich and I visited poor Veksler. Following the conversation with Klokov he had fallen ill with depression. Emes had indeed been publishing his poetry and he knew the editors there very well . . . But this wasn't the point. It was all this infamous anti-semitic campaign which had been fabricated on purpose and propagated artificially. He lay on the divan in crumpled pyjamas. Pages of verses were strewn all over the place and his service jacket with its decoration hung shapeless and dejected on the back of a chair. Lying there, Veksler was thumbing through the sheets and chewing his pencil. It was clear that he was trying to make some positive sense of what was going on. I remembered trying too, once, to make it all comprehensible and acceptable.

"After all, we don't know everything," he said and sighed. "It's difficult for us to judge what is right and what is not right from the point of view of international politics. There, at the top, they see things more clearly. Their horizons are broader. From Stalin's viewpoint one can see the whole world . . . Take the home guard for example. I couldn't understand at the time why it was necessary to throw into the battle untrained, unarmed men. After all how many members of the intelligentsia perished in those days. They might have proved valuable. And only several years later did I realize the brilliance of Stalin's plan for the defence of Moscow. Stalin threw into the battle untrained men to give time for the reserves to be brought up. And Moscow was saved.

"And the destruction of Emes is also essential to save Moscow?" I wanted to ask, but didn't. "And the slanderous remarks about the critics? And the fomenting of anti-semitism?"

But I held my peace. I didn't argue. Bilibin explained to me very clearly the why's and the wherefore's and, in any case, I knew myself how senseless and risky it was to argue about such subjects. For instance, what on earth was the point of arguing with a blockhead like Klokov? It was both dangerous and hopeless.

"He wouldn't understand anything in any case," Bilibin pointed out to me. "And he might take it into his head to go and write a denunciation. 'On such and such a date, in such and such a place in the presence of so and so, the above-mentioned person uttered unpatriotic thoughts and expressed mistrust of the Party press.' And they'll start pulling us old dears in, Sergei Dimitrievich and myself, as witnesses. . . . I can see myself giving evidence against you!" he concluded with a laugh. "No, Nina Sergeievna, for heaven's sake you mustn't be so indiscreet. Think of yourself and us sinners too. You mustn't do it."

Bilibin himself, so it turned out, had ended up in a camp because of some careless remark made in the company of friends, someone had informed on him—and so it began . . . the whole group was pulled in. If one of them proved obstinate, two would confirm what had been said. And a life was broken.

Veksler, of course, was another matter, one could talk to him without being afraid, but Nikolai Aleksandrovich kept asking what was the point in trying to prevent a person from finding a profound and mysterious meaning in evil humbug, if thereby, he found it easier to preserve his peace of mind? One should leave him alone.

In any case, we didn't stay long in Veksler's room. His desire to talk to me alone was much too apparent. I got up. He jumped off the divan in his pyjamas and socks. Sheets of paper flew onto the floor. He hastily picked them up.

"I don't need social visits," he said to me gloomily, crouching on all fours and looking up at me from the ground. "I want to see you alone to read you some new poems . . ."

Of course I felt sorry for Veksler and was prepared to listen to his poetry, but Klokov simply made me feel sick. At lunch he once told us himself how he had learnt to shoot when he was a child, about twelve years old. He used to tie a cat to a tree and fire. "Because when it moved, jumped or ran it was difficult to hit," he explained. "Not bad training for the profession of critic," I thought. . . . His discussion of poetry made me choke with laughter and rage.

"The classics aren't all good," he came out with yesterday. "Nekrasov for instance, wrote, 'In the forest the woodman's axe resounded.' Actually, it's not correct to say that. It was the thudding that resounded and not the axe. But we forgive Nekrasov because he's a classic."

At lunch today he gave us a whole lecture on love.

"Our leading organizations," he informed us, "have explained that our press—our literature—" he corrected himself, "have been wrong in devoting insufficient attention to problems of love. It's time the feeling of love took its rightful place in life and literature. The classics of Marxism were not against love. Up till now we have not taken due account of the fact that love increases our energy and this energy lends wings to men, enabling them to perform great deeds which, in their turn, can be exploited for the building of communism. . . . Marx, Engels and Lenin thought highly of love for the very reason that it stimulates . . ."

"Nina Sergeievna," Bilibin implored me, as we were going up the stairs together after lunch, "let's go and dig ditches! I suddenly feel an eccess of energy! It must be exploited."

I doubled up with laughter and had difficulty in reaching my room . . .

It was now evening. I sat down and waited for Bilibin. He was bound to come. The power-station thumped away, counting off our minutes together. The electric lights grew brighter, dimmer, brighter again. I was waiting for the familiar footsteps and trying to read *Hatter's Castle*. But somehow I couldn't concentrate on the reading. Yesterday I saw the place where Lyolka lived. It was far more interesting than any castle. I had taken with me a pie, sweets, which they used to give us for tea, and a book of Russian fairy-tales, which happened to be in the library.

There were nine tiny houses in Bykovo in all—there had been thirty but the Germans had burnt them in 1941. There were wooden fences, mud, scraggy goats with some sort of dishevelled tow instead of woollen coats. In the house where Lyolka lived I saw dirty rags, dirty earthenware pots and a round loudspeaker which blared away above the rags and unwashed children. The room looked as though burglars had just been there, had removed everything, and had thrown the remaining trash all over the place. On the floor lay a fragment of a mirror, on the table greasy pillows without covers. Lyolka, bare-footed and dishevelled, was staggering round the room with the year-old Vitka, tossing him up higher, but he would keep slipping down. "Relying on the immense aid of party and government," said the round loudspeaker, when I went in, "in equipping agriculture with machinery in the current year in an unprecedentedly short space of time . . ." I turned the radio off, sat the baby on the bed and shoved a sweet in its mouth. I gave Lyolka one and started to read her a fairy-story. How attentively she listened! With arms, eyebrows, knees rubbing against one another in impatience and with open mouth. She put a piece of pie in her mouth and forgot to chew and swallow. One story was about the feather of Finist the clear-eyed hawk, another about a wicked princess who stole a magic pipe from a poor shepherd boy by deceiving him.

"Finist, the clear-eyed hawk came flying at midnight and beat his wings against the window, beat and beat but only wounded himself all over until he was covered with blood and had cut his wings.

'Farewell, lovely maiden,' he said sadly, 'I am flying off to the other end of the world, to a kingdom beyond the seas. If you love me look for me there. When you have worn out three pairs of iron shoes, broken three iron staves and gnawed through three iron loaves you will find me.'

Thus he spoke and soared into the sky.

And though the maid could hear these ungracious words as she slept she hadn't the strength to open her eyes."

I finished the story and prepared to hurry home for my treatment.

"Had I this little book," said Lyolka as she accompanied me to the door with the baby in her arms, "I would not go to bed, I would read it! Night and day I would read it without closing my eyes!"

I was struck again how much her words sounded in

tune with the fairy-tale.

"But you can't even read."

"I shall learn to read! I already know the letter 'F'."

I started to put on my over-shoes. Lyolka drew the baby up higher.

"Were I a princess," she said in singsong voice, like a peasant woman telling a fairy story, "I would not be wicked. . . . I would not have taken his pipe away from him, I would have blown on it once—just for fun . . . I would have had pity on the shepherd-boy who brought me the pipe . . ."

. . . March 1949

We were sitting on tree-trunks in a forest glade. I had put my muff on a stump and he his warm cap. There was no wind and the sun already felt warm. The forest wore its winter garments but the deep blue shadows and the pale blue sky already heralded spring. The snow was soft today. What a pity I was no good as a sculptor.

He was sitting, hatless, with his coat thrown open and head thrown back, gazing at the sky. And once again his face looked different. It was still as though without expression, but his eyes were restless. And the wind ruffled the thinning hair over his high forehead.

He took a handful of snow and kneaded it.

"Put your cap on, you'll catch cold," I said.

"Do you know that Veksler is in love with you?" Bilibin asked, instead of answering.

"So what!"

"I suppose you think that that's something easy and pleasant?"

"I don't think about him at all. I don't think about

him ever."

"Do you think about me?"

"A lot."

"He says that you are poetry itself, that you are art itself, and heaven knows what else."

"There's no accounting for the nonsense some people talk. I'm just not interested."

Nikolai Aleksandrovich got up, put on his cap, lit a cigarette and took a few steps over the glade. From the stump he walked to a pine-tree, from the pine-tree back to the stump. Then he flung his cigarette a long way away and came up to me from behind. He lifted the collar of my coat and the soft fur tickled my cheeks and ears. He lightly tipped my head back so that I could see his shaven chin from below, his lips and his intent, shining eyes, lowered to look at me.

I shook my head vigorously in the palm of his hands.

He lowered his arms and walked away and I adjusted my collar. Then he stopped right in front of me, screening me from the fir-trees and the sky. At that moment he seemed very tall.

"Please tell me why I may not kiss you!"

What could I reply? I didn't know why myself. Perhaps I hadn't liked the business-like, preliminary gesture with which he had flung away the cigarette . . . I didn't know.

I got up and brushed my coat. We walked home in silence. I noticed that the fir-trees in the heavy snow looked like large, white triangles. Bilibin's face looked angry. "And indeed, why had I said no?" I thought. "I had only spoiled the walk. But then I wasn't entirely to blame . . . Or rather not only myself . . . After all, it didn't depend entirely on my will . . . whether to or not to . . ."

"So you won't reveal to me the state secret?" Bilibin asked, ironically.

"Don't be angry with me, Nikolai Aleksandrovich," I said. "It's difficult to explain. Herzen said somewhere: 'Words often fall short'."*

Not far from the rest-home we met Lyudmila Pavlovna. I had already seen her after she had returned that morning. She had not found out anything about her sister. "The Public Prosecutor's office was jammed with people and one could get no sense out of them." But when she returned she had found a telegram on her table from somewhere in the north. Her sister asked her to send candles, matches, sugar . . . she was living in a mud hut. "Thank heavens," I said. "If she can send a telegram, she can't be in a camp."

"Do you think anyone could have seen the telegram?" Lyudmila Pavlovna had asked me in reply.

Now, however, she greeted us with a polite smile and enveloped us with a fragrant scent.

"It's just like a fairy story in the forest today," she said, adjusting her fluffy shawl. "Just like the Bolshoi Theatre."

Against his wont, Bilibin did not kiss both her hands or assure her that she was as slim as a palm-tree.

"Why did Veksler make you his confidant?" I asked as we approached the house. "What was the reason?"

"Evidently he looks upon me as his successful rival. And feels he has the right to grumble and complain . . ."

We climbed up the steps to the house. I led the way.

"And you," I asked, turning to face him. Our eyes were level.

"What do you mean—me?"

"You yourself, do you look upon yourself as his successful rival?"

"Rival, yes, but as you should know, not particularly successful . . .'Words often fall short'," he mocked me with ill-concealed spite. "Must you always be serious and always quote somebody or other? . . ."

Opening the heavy door for me he started flicking the snow off his hunting boots with birch twigs.

At lunch and at supper he had been unusually curt with me. And after supper, instead of coming to my room as he usually did, sitting down on a low bench and answering my questions by silence or with some fresh horrible detail, he went straight into the guest room. And it seemed to me from where I was that I could see his large hands, dealing out the cards. From time to time his self-assured voice reached my ears. I wanted to cry. May God forgive him! How wonderful it had been two weeks ago. I hadn't cared whether he was sitting in the guest-room or not. He had been a stranger. He could sit where he wanted. And I could go to the grove alone and not wonder how I would tell him that I had seen a purple-grey circle over the birch-trees; I could make my descent and read poetry and examine people and write letters . . . But now?

And now my loneliness was full of him.

How impatiently he had thrown away the cigarette in the glade . . . Would he forgive me what had happened today?

. . . But why and how had we suddenly started talking in such a stupid way: 'rival', 'successful rival', 'unsuccessful rival'. 'Rival' in what? How could we have degraded what we had experienced together by using those trite words?

Man is a 'system enclosed within itself' and each person is alone in his own system. And suddenly it is as though the forehead is opened up and one can see what lies behind the forehead, behind . . .

And after such a miracle he had dared to say that he was not happy! That evening on the footpath and the moment when he talked for the first time, after the heart attack? Those two weeks when we exchanged memories every day? And he was not happy!

. . . *March 1949*

I woke up in the night from a sudden glare of light in my eyes. I lifted my head and a broad white band of light lay on the seat of the chair then switched to the wall and disappeared.

What was it?

I heard the sharp snap of a door downstairs.

A car! Someone had driven up to the house in a car. It was the headlights.

The power station didn't work a night. I had nothing to use as a light. I could only lie in complete darkness and listen.

I heard the discreet hiss of the front door opening and another hiss as it closed.

That meant they were already inside the house.

But whom had they come to see? To fetch?

There were no footsteps. At any rate on our floor. Perhaps it was nothing but a dream?

A deep, absolute silence pervaded the house. But ten minutes later I heard the hiss of the door again in the hall downstairs. I jumped up and ran to the window. I drew the curtains aside. It was pitch black but I could clearly hear the starting of a car. And a light—dull and faint—made the hoar-frost on my window seem silvery. Someone was going down the steps with a lamp. Three

—no, four—dark figures could be seen. Again a car-door slammed. The engine was running and the bright headlights shone on the snow.

And that was all. The lamp rose jerkily up the steps of the house and the door hissed once more.

It must have been Lyudmila Pavlovna with the lamp. The director was in town today.

She was living in the little Finnish house for the staff and not here in ours. They might have called for her there and brought her to our house. After all, someone had to open the door, light the lamp and show them the room! Noiselessly. Quietly.

Whose room?

No, it wasn't room No. 8, not No. 8 because there had been no footsteps along our corridor.

Downstairs were the rooms of the science-fiction writer, Veksler, Valentina Nikolayevna, the adventure story writer, Sergei Dimitriyevich . . .

That night I saw the window grow pale, heard the stokers go down to the boiler-room, the hum of the steam central-heating as it started up and the first hesitant thump emitted by the power station.

I got up at seven o'clock and went down to the bathroom in the basement. I thought that if I had a thorough wash I would feel better. But however much I rubbed my face, shoulders, arms I felt as though they were covered with a cobweb of darkness and sleeplessness.

The face of an old hag looked out at me from the mirror.

I hoped to meet Lyudmila Pavlovna somewhere—she would tell me the truth. The box had brought us closer together. I walked down the corridor several times and glanced into the guest-room. She wasn't there. Should I go to the store house to find Tonya? No, she would be unlikely to know. In any case what did she care? . . . Who were we to her? She had no time to read our books and, if she did, she wouldn't believe a word. We were strangers, useless people for whom one had to work. Masters. "Writers".

"Writers, put down the receiver" the switchboard operator would say when connecting someone.

"The writers have a cinema."

"Has the post already been delivered to the writers?"

At exactly nine o'clock I went down to breakfast.

Bilibin, dressed all in black, pale with bluish lips, was standing by the table. His large hands rested on the back of a chair.

I approached. We stood facing one another. I was grateful to him that he had not kept me waiting another minute.

"So it wasn't you?" I said. "No, it wasn't you. It wasn't you."

"You were afraid for me?"

"Yes."

"Say: I was afraid for you," he begged in a whisper.

"I was afraid for you," I repeated.

"Give me your hand . . . Shall I tell you?"

There was something insistent in his question and the yellow glance which he directed at me . . . His hand felt cold and strong.

"Veksler."

The poor sheets of poetry, the pathetic decoration, the poor grey innocent head! Poor Lyutik.

I couldn't eat. I was shivering. Fortunately there was nobody else in the dining-room as yet. Bilibin made me drink some hot coffee. We went up the staircase together and together we went to my room.

"He was a good man," said Bilibin with obvious

sympathy.

The 'was' made me cry. Again the past tense although the man was still alive! Bilibin gently stroked my hair.

"Please leave me," I said. "I must lie down."

He left.

And I lay down. I would not get up today. My heart was pounding relentlessly and my face ached from my tears. I wrote lying in bed.

. . . March 1949

The whole morning we wandered round the birch forest. The tops of the birch-trees were bathing in the blue sky, high overhead. It was spacious and light in the forest as it was in our house. Today, so it seemed, was the most meaningful of our walks. We had already learned to be silent together. We were silent about the night, about Veksler, about second-timers and about the impossibility of living through something like 1937 again.

We sat for a while on a bench and gazed at the snowy plain and the roofs of the houses of Bykovo. Then we wandered home. The whole time the thought of whether I should show him 'Street Lamps', whether to tear it out of my diary and show him, was gnawing at me . . .

I decided I would do it only after he had finished his own work. After all, somebody else's writing hinders one's own.

After a bath and a meal I fell asleep. When I woke up I began to search, as I always did at such a moment, for the chink of light shining from under the door. No, there was no light. And I couldn't hear the thump of the power-station, although it always began to pulse after half-past four. Perhaps I had woken up earlier than usual. No, the house was on its feet. There was a heavy movement, some kind of confusion, people talking, running to and fro and the discreet banging of doors.

Knocking against chairs in the dark, I felt for my dressing-gown and looked out into the corridor. It was dark in the corridor, too. Only a tiny square of window showed white at the end. And suddenly through the window something pink flickered and disappeared in the snow. Like the flap of a wing.

I went to the window.

Right in front of me the little Finnish house was blazing like a fierce towering bonfire. The soft, pink glow of the flame was reflected in the shroud of snow.

"You're up? I was on my way to wake you," Bilibin said to me, soundlessly approaching the window, in his soft slippers. "It's only been burning fifteen minutes and there's practically nothing left." He took my hand in his. We stood by the window. Our shoulders touching. "Fire-brigade, indeed. You have to go thirty kilometres for the nearest! It burnt in a trice . . . The local youth rushed here from Bykovo, from Kuzminskoe, gaily shouting: 'The writers are on fire!' You don't believe me? It's true. And nobody lifted a finger. They just stood and stared. . . . A stove started it."

"There were no people there? In the house?"

"No. Only things."

He spoke slowly, with a kind of drawl and settled down on the window-sill without releasing my hand, as though that was the way things should be on the occasion of the fire.

The pink glow suddenly suffused his shoulders and chest, his large head and my hand, resting in his. He didn't move but only squeezed my hand more firmly.

"Whose things are there?"

"The nurse's, Lyudmila Pavlovna's. She's crying and promises to make the nurse who left the stove on pay the cost."

I found it pleasant to stand and gaze at the fire, to listen to him and submit myself to the pressure of his hand, and also a little frightening perhaps from the dark and the sudden leaping of the flames.

"They really shouted: 'The writers are on fire'?" I asked.

"Yes."

"Did Lyolka, too?"

He didn't answer. The pink glow was already fading, as though absorbed by the snow. Darkness was falling outside the windows. The little house had finished burning.

"When they put the lights on again I'll bring you my story," Bilibin said. "I finished it whilst you were asleep. There."

And he took my hand and playfully made me stroke his hair.

. . . March 1949

I read it through.

Yesterday we had been standing at the window side by side. Together.

It was the usual, typewritten manuscript. But I would never forget the type, never forget the lilac colour of the ribbon and the ornate seven in the numbering of the chapters.

I would never forget a single word.

At first I recognized everything and rejoiced at it all.

The sounds of the forest. The sounds of the mine, under-neath the earth, in the dark. Time down below and in the forest. The hum of the lift in the mine. The quiet of the tenth level. Yes, his writing was more powerful than his conversation . . . And I began to recognize people.

Sasha Sokolyansky, for instance. Here he was called Boltyansky—a handsome, clever man—and his stuttering made him especially attractive. Sasha was a miner in the story. And who was that with the wooden laugh? Ah yes, that must have been inspired by the guard—the one who didn't let the prisoners sleep on purpose. He had the same wooden laugh . . . Here he was an engineer and, evidently, a saboteur . . . There was also a child in the story, frail and sickly, but that was because he was tor-mented by a family quarrel. And the main hero, the miner, Peter, I somehow couldn't place him at all. There was no such person in what he had told me. And the subject matter. . . . Well, of course, he couldn't very well write about the camp for *Znamya* . . . But then why use those mountains, that forest, those people . . . There was even the incident with the letter—somebody read over again a letter from his wife and the wind ripped the sheet of paper away and he perished. It wasn't a dog, however, that flung itself on him but he himself who stumbled into a ditch as he chased after the letter.

The gangs of miners competed with one another. The victory over the fascists led to a big rise in labour pro-ductivity. The miner, Peter, returned from the front to his wife, Fedosya. She had worked before on the lift in the mine and during the war had matured ideologically and professionally like millions of Soviet women, whose shoulders bore the burden of the economy of the country. She had stuck it out! There were a lot of such colloquial words in the story. Whilst Peter fought, she had worked, educated the children and studied. She became an engineer and struggled hard to introduce modern machinery. She not only took her gang off picks and put them on drills but took a trip to Moscow and got hold of a coal-cutting machine. The clever machine, cut, loaded and did the transport work all by itself. They had worked like granddad for long enough! Fedosya was very good at conducting propaganda. Peter was dissatisfied. He had grown used to the pick and didn't want to have to change his ideas. The decorations had turned his head. Not only that, but he was quite needlessly jealous of the chief engineer whom his wife didn't actually like at all. On the contrary, she was the first to unmask his wrecking activities . . .

Euphoria reigned in the pit. The miners got up early for a pre-October anniversary shift but in Peter's home there was discord and almost violence. His sickly five-year-old son said to Peter: "Daddy, don't you touch my Mum or I shall write to comrade Stalin. He'll take up the cudgels on our behalf. He won't let a working woman be hurt." After one such family scene the child ran off to see the Party official, falling and stumbling in a blizzard on his tiny, frail legs. The official tried to make Peter see reason but he proved stubborn. Then the official told the peasant woman Marya (she had lost four sons in the war) to have a heart-to-heart talk with him. The old woman found the right words to touch Peter to the core and he went home and asked Fedosya for forgiveness.

"His fingers trembled as he rolled a piece of paper to make a cigarette. . . . 'Fedosya, my dearest!' he said in a hollow voice, 'I'm to blame! Forgive the old fool. I've been led astray. The old woman brought me to my senses.' "

When I had finished reading I closed the manuscript

and sat at the desk for a long time, gazing at the neat folder. "Nikolai Bilibin" had been inscribed on it in distinct round letters. "Fedosya's Victory. A Tale."

So this was what he had been writing from seven o'clock in the morning. This was why he had come here, to be quiet. This was the memorial he had raised to the memory of his friend. This was what he wanted to tell Tonya and Lyolka, Veksler and Lyudmila Pavlovna.

Up till now I had often experienced grief in my life. But this was the first time that I felt shame.

My feeling of shame was so strong that time came to a stop. Just as it does when one is happy.

I didn't hear any footsteps. There was a knock on the door. I knew that it was Bilibin. He always knocked lightly, and carefully, with the very tips of his nails. As though he walked on tiptoe.

I didn't immediately react to the knock. I had to collect myself and my voice.

"Come in," I said, at length. "Do sit down."

I motioned him to a chair on the other side of the desk. In my room he had always sat beside me on a little bench. He showed surprise, but sat down.

"You're a coward," I said. "No, worse, you're a false witness." He started to get up. "You're a liar. You're pretentious, you're an old woman. . ."

He got up and straightened himself. Without taking his eyes off me he stretched out his hand towards the table and groped for the file.

"His fingers trembled as he rolled a piece of paper to make a cigarette," I said and got up myself. "That's all. You can go. That's all I can tell you about your writings . . . Goodbye. Why did you not have the decency to remain silent? Merely remain silent? After all no-one demanded this from you . . . Do you mean to say . . .

out of respect for those . . . whom you buried in the earth . . . you couldn't earn your bread and butter in some other way? Doing something else? Instead of at the expense of the forest. Or the mine. Or the child from there. Or . . . the stuttering of your friend?"

He left the room.

. . . *March 1949*

How was I to go back to the grove, to that same grove where I had gone on the first day? That benign grove that had given me the gift of peace? Now I no longer had reason to be grateful to it.

Now, however much I asked, it gave me nothing. Today it was all covered with frozen, glittering snow. But because I had filled the grove with something else it was no longer a consolation, it was no longer inhabited by silence.

In some ways I had done wrong, and it had deprived me of its consolation.

It was too late to repent or appeal to it for help. The day after tomorrow I was leaving.

How would I be able to live through these two days under the same roof as Nikolai Aleksandrovich? Have dinner, breakfast . . . And then travel together as well . . . But it seems he was ill. . .

This morning I entered the dining-room with a beating heart. But only Sergei Dimitriyevich was sitting at the table. Bilibin was not there.

"Our worthy colleague is ill again. Have you been to see him?" Sergei Dimitriyevich asked me. "If you go and see him give him my best wishes. I shall visit him, too. The nurse said that his heart is poorly again."

"Oh, is that so? No, I haven't been to see him yet."

I went for a walk three times today. Forty-five minutes each time. Exactly. By the clock. Without indulging myself.

After lunch I went to meet Lyolka. At this time of the day she usually left her little brother with neighbours and popped round to the station for bread. I met her, took her bag from her, thrust some pies, apples and chocolate into it and walked with her almost to the village.

"Is there a river in Moscow?" Lyolka asked.

"Yes, there is. The river Moscow. It's deep."

"How deep? Up to where?"

"I don't know. Bathing is forbidden in the city."

"What's the use of the river then?"

The skinny, sharp-eyed, agile child hid her red, frozen hands under her black shawl.

"You're going to Moscow soon?"

"Soon, Lyolka, very soon."

"Will you take me with you?"

She stopped, blew on her hands and looked at me with her large eyes.

"Lyolka! How on earth can I take you with me? Your mother is here. She wouldn't part with her daughter."

"Yes, she would! She'll say: 'Clear out, Lyolka, clear out! A fat lot of use you are to me! You're just another mouth to feed!' I could do everything for you . . . I can wash up and iron your ribbons for you."

She stood, looking at me and rubbing her nose so hard with her sleeve that it seemed as if she wanted to rub it away altogether.

I arranged her shawl and crouched down, blowing on her red hands to make them warm.

"I shall send you some mittens. I won't forget. I shall

write to you and send you a book. Later on you shall come and stay with us—with me and Katya."

I gave her back her bag. She turned round and ran off towards the village—a little scarecrow of a girl. Her bag was flapping round her legs.

"Which story will you send me? The Wing of the Clear-Eyed Hawk? And the one about the pipe?" she shouted, turning round once again.

I wanted to catch her up, make the sign of the cross over her and whisper something loving like "God bless you!" I said quietly to myself: "Run along my little princess, I shall not forget about you."

I walked back over the fields and went down towards the stream. After all, I had to say goodbye to the stream. It was not frozen but was cooing like a dove.

When I got back I settled myself at my desk and forced myself to work on the translation. In the end it was all a question of will-power. An old Jewish woman in a hospital once told me: "The main thing is to keep a firm grip on oneself." I forced myself to work, but not for long. Because I could see through the walls: along the corridor beyond the guest-room there was a room and a man was lying in it with blue lips, propped up on pillows, gazing at the door. I once calculated that there were nineteen steps from his door to mine.

But now they had turned into nineteen kilometres. No less. Into nineteen centuries.

. . . March 1949

Tomorrow I was leaving. The time in my room seemed different because tomorrow was the last day. It didn't drag and it didn't fly. It simply didn't exist. It had been pumped out as air is sometimes pumped out.

I was no longer sitting in my own room, but in someone else's. It was no longer the home I had yearned for for so long, but simply a room in a hotel in which someone else would be living the day after tomorrow. And the curtains were no longer anyone's—they were alien, not mine. It had simply become a small waiting-room like a station, for instance.

Today, I didn't feel like walking, or working, or getting out of my dressing-gown for lunch. And I could have lain like that on the divan without doing anything. What did it matter? Tomorrow was the end in any case . . . However, lunch came, and the rest-hour and the chink of light under the door and the sunset in its usual place—everything as it had been twenty-five times. And I even saw Bilibin again.

I saw him, but he didn't see me. I had been walking in the morning. I had not gone a very long way—only as far as the fir-trees. We had rarely been there together . . . I sat down on a damp, half-frozen tree-stump and pulled the edges of my coat over my knees. He was walking by himself along the path, his cap in his pocket and his face turned towards the warm wind. Was he coming here? Had he seen me? I felt my heart constrict from emotion, or perhaps, happiness. No, he wasn't coming this way. Thick, broad fir-trees separated us. He was walking slowly, with difficulty. From time to time he tore away the moss from the trunks and crushed it between the palms of his hands. In the bright daylight I could see his face down to the smallest details: the yellow eyes, bluish lips and dark web of wrinkles. The wind ruffled the thin air on his high forehead as it had then in the glade. And I suddenly remembered him touching his head with my hand on the day of the fire, remembered how soft his hair was, like a child's! How easily the wind played through it now. He was walking along, thinking of something or other and mechanically crushing the moss between his palms when all of a sudden he stopped. His large hand felt for the button on his chest, he undid it and pulled from his inside pocket—I knew what it was —nitroglycerine! He pulled out the tiny cork with a pin, tipped a few grains onto his palm and took one with his lips . . . He stood for a while, aware of the pain, and turning round slowly made his way back—home. The wind was rumpling his hair now—not over his forehead but at the back of his neck . . . He had probably gone to lie down.

"Put your hat on, or you'll catch cold," I wanted to say as I had then. "Stop a little, don't hurry, let the pain go away," I wanted to say, as I had said many times when out for a walk. "Forgive me!" I wanted to say. "I didn't have the right to judge you; least of all I, for no dogs ever threw themselves on me and I've never seen the wooden tag on the leg of a dead man . . . Forgive me! You wouldn't wish to go back there: to felling trees, to the mines. Go back for a second time! The story you wrote is your weak shield, your unreliable wall . . . Forgive me! You've already had one heart attack—illness is expensive and you need your earnings. And how else can you earn money as a sick man? Only by writing. Writing lies like a hack . . . Forgive me! I didn't have the right to demand the truth from you. I'm healthy and yet I keep silent. I was never beaten at night in the investigator's room. And when they beat you I kept silent. What right have I then to judge you now? Forgive me my cursed cruelty, forgive me!"

Should I run after him—call him—tell him?

I sat without moving, trying as hard as I could to pull

the ends of my coat over my knees, and all the time, slowly and inevitably, Bilibin moved further away.

He was going out of my life.

For the first time I saw his back, his gait, his powerful shoulders and his weak faltering legs which seemed to give way beneath him. He picked his way slowly and uncertainly, his legs bearing his big body—the broad shoulders and large head—unsteadily . . .

I felt sorry for him, and I felt sorry for myself, and for everyone. "Russia, my motherland," I thought in someone else's words. Bilibin's slow-moving shoulders gradually disappeared behind the trees. It was still possible to catch him up, call him, ask him for forgiveness, he was still here; we were still together . . .

Goodbye! Goodbye for ever!

. . . As dusk was falling I again went out for a stroll, unable to bear the room that was no longer mine. There was no frost, no snow. It was thawing, melting. Mud clung to my shoes. I went back, put on my galoshes and for all that walked squelching to the grove. To our house. The snow was still lying there as before, but it reeked of damp. The jackdaws were croaking. On all sides there was a whispering, a dripping, activity. The snowdrifts had caved in; their dark surface was pitted with holes, nostrils. The grove was untidy today. The snow on the branches was spread out carelessly, in dirty lumps—like cotton-wool on a discarded Christmas tree. "It is washing away our old tracks and that's fine," I thought. I slipped on a clinging lump of earth and almost fell. One leg sunk in. I dragged it out with difficulty and kicked the sticky lump away from me.

When I die I shall become just such a clod, and so will he. Despite everything that has been written, said, thought about it, it's impossible to understand. One's hands and one's eyes and one's mouth will become earth. One's memory. Anxiety. Sins. Truth. And falsehood.

And when this finally comes to pass they will feel no pain if someone steps on the clods of earth.

. . . March 1949. Moscow

At 11 o'clock, after I had had breakfast the snub-nosed nurse carried my case out to the car. Lyudmila Pavlovna came out onto the steps to see me off. Bilibin had also got ready to travel, which meant that he had not fallen ill after all.

He had survived. Thank God!

To say goodbye, Lyudmila Pavlovna took me to one side. "Oh, what . . . an original . . . scarf you have. . . . You can see at once it's not ours . . . It can't be from Mostorg? Please, Nina Sergeyevna," she squeezed my hand, "please don't say a word to anyone . . . you don't mean to say you got it without queueing? Well, I must say, you were jolly lucky . . . Come and see us again, won't you?"

Fortunately Bilibin and I were not travelling alone. I got in next to the driver, and the fat man with high blood pressure settled down next to Nikolai Aleksandrovich on the back seat. His pressure had gone down to 160 and he was going home to his Yasha, very pleased . . . I wondered what Yasha would tell him? (When I was at school we didn't know what anti-semitism meant. We had grown used to regarding it as something ridiculous, old-fashioned, out of date—something rather like a halbard for instance).

. . . The snow was still melting like yesterday. Only the branches had been lightly dusted with hoar-frost and the road powdered with snow. The fields, the birch-trees, the hills up which the fir-trees clambered, flew to meet me—as well as the purple splash of the road.

Behind me in the back of the car the men were smoking and quietly talking. Bilibin's voice was, as usual, calm, amiable. I wasn't listening to them. I would like to have jumped out, gone back to the grove just once more to see the birch-trees dancing round the firs. To see the nursery school growing green from beneath its white blanket. To call in my room before it became completely alien and glance through its clear windows.

It was too late. That would never ever be again. I could already see the station.

We had arrived! The driver lifted out the fat man's briefcase, my light case and Bilibin's heavy one and put them on the platform. He bought tickets, distributed them to us and hurriedly collected his tips. The train came in. There was a crush and scramble. It was stifling. The driver dragged the cases into the carriage, put the briefcase on the rack and the trunks under the seats. "Have a good journey!" and jumped out.

The train moved off.

I sat down in the corner and closed my eyes. Ilya Isaakovich and Bilibin were solving some chess problem, bent over the magazine *Ogonyok*. Their voices merged with the knocking of the wheels and other voices.

The over-heated carriage was filled with women sitting, motionless, next to their milk-cans and sacks; with old peasant women; snotty-nosed kids; railway workers; disabled soldiers; some young drunk, lying face down on the seat, with the top of his white-haired head sticking up; and some young black-browed girls with painted lips in green knitted berets and yellow mittens.

They had all come a long way and, apart from the sleeping youth, were telling each other in enormous detail their stories which must have been begun some stations back.

"She pinched and scoffed four of my pullets. The feathers she shoved in a trunk. That's where I found them. I took two mouldy old pillows off her and a samovar—a bit of old iron—for the hens she pinched."

'We celebrated the marriage in the autumn. It'll be fine if they give him a permit to live in the village. The only thing is one needs some pull with the militia . . "

"Our Zinaida married an old 'un. He's a foreman on the railway. She married him for a room. Her son from her first husband is in a children's home. So when the old man dies she can take her son home. She's a mother after all, she must see that they've got somewhere to live . . ."

"I called at the local clinic. The doctors didn't know what it was. Then I went to a private clinic and saw a professor. He said it's nothing, too. It's on nervous grounds. What the devil do they mean by 'nervous grounds', that's what I'd like to know. Whenever it rains my back hurts like hell."

The words "Russia, my motherland," came back to me. I surreptitiously began to scrutinize the other passengers.

What sort of people were they? What went on inside? How could I glance within and make contact with them? What lay behind these chickens . . . the private clinic . . . the wedding . . . What did each of them see in their darkness when they closed their eyes to go to sleep? If only I could go under with them and see what they saw. That would really be a descent. Taking them with me. Getting into their memory. Well, at least into the memories of the people of this carriage.

"I was told to go to the school on Thursday. You've spoiled him they said. But to my thinking the teacher is too young and unsure of herself. The children play her up and that's just what he does . . ."

"Mind you, I won't say they're wealthy, but they've got more than us to live on. They were selling bottled fruit before the holiday—not ours but Bulgarian—and I'll tell you, she took five kilos . . . Everyone else just got one and there she was carrying off five . . . think what you like . . . "

An hour later the train left the bright light of day and entered the half light of Moscow station.

The women slung their bags on their shoulders and picked up their cans.

The fat man tied the ginger-coloured scarf round his neck and, with eyes popping, took his briefcase down from the rack. Bilibin buttoned his coat up and made sure he had the nitroglycerine in his pocket. He seized my case just as I was about to take it down.

I am not going to argue, I thought. The case is empty and light.

A middle-aged lady, with an attractive face, skilfully made-up, came up to us on the platform. Bilibin kissed her hand. "Of course, the wife," I recalled. "Marina Avgustinovna. He told me that he got married when he returned. She was working in a Savings Bank if I remember rightly."

"Let me introduce you, Marina," Bilibin said, looking anxiously, first at her then at me. "This was my charming neighbour, Nina Sergeievna, I told you so much about her in my letters. And this is the Ilya Isaakovich with whom I played chess . . . Well, what do you think? Do I look better?"

"Very glad to meet you," said Marina and I saw that

139

she knew how to turn on a smile just as well as he did. "Darling! You mustn't carry heavy weights. The doctor expressly forbade it."

Without more to-do she took my case from him and carried it herself.

I didn't protest. I should have done, but I couldn't be bothered. "Let her carry it, if she likes to. It doesn't matter," I thought.

Bilibin hailed a taxi in the square. The fat man with high blood pressure said goodbye to us. He lived close by and had no luggage. Bilibin opened the car-door for me and I got in . . . Let him take me!

"Where can we drop you?" Marina Avgustinovna asked me with the same agreeable smile. It's very easy to smile like that: one just bares one's teeth and slightly screws up one's eyes. I gave the driver my address.

The couple travelled in silence waiting for me to get out.

We reached Mayakovsky square, then Pushkin square . . . There was no snow in the city . . . in the grove the snow had been white, here everything looked black.

In five minutes I would be home, if one could call it home. Home to Katya. No, she would still be at school. To Elizaveta Nikolaievna.

The car stopped at the front entrance.

Bilibin got out, took my case and opened the door of the car.

"Allow me, allow me, it's nothing . . . Let me help you with it up the steps. Thank you for your company. Say hello for me to your little daughter. I can imagine how she's longing to see you again! She'll come home from school and find her Mummy at home. What a lovely surprise! Well, all the very best! Keep well!"

1949–1957

NOTES

of the greatest dancers of her day.

Anna Akhmatova (1888–1967): One of the greatest Russian poets of the twentieth century. She suffered much persecution during the Stalin era. For many years she was a personal friend of Lydia Chukovskaya.

38 *Writers' Union*: an official organization representing writers. It ensures their ideological and political conformity. During the Great Purge and the "anti-cosmopolitan" campaign of 1949–50 the Union played a dominant part in supporting the vilification of its own members by the Party.

Sovietsky Pisatel': Publishing house founded in 1938 to popularize Soviet fiction, drama and poetry.

45 The confiscation of the property of an arrested person is practised under Soviet penal law. Such confiscation assumed considerable proportions during the Great Purge and in the postwar period of repression.

46 A grim monument to the ferocity and bitterness of the siege of Leningrad in the Second World War are the communal graves in the Piskaryovskoye cemetery.

51 *Emes* (The Truth): publishing house specializing in Yiddish literature, which was closed down in November 1948.

Novy Mir (New World): A monthly literary journal and organ of the Writers' Union, founded in 1925. It has represented, particularly after the death of Stalin and under the editorship of Tvardovsky, a more liberal approach in Russian literature and literary criticism.

Znamya (Banner): A monthly literary journal with a more conservative approach than *Novy Mir*.

53 *Theatrical Society*: The All-Russian Theatrical Society for actors, actresses, film-directors, pro-

ducers, etc.

55 Lines from Nekrasov's "Red-Nosed Frost".

57 *Yesenin* (1895–1925): A Russian poet of peasant origin who had great lyrical gifts. He became disenchanted with the outcome of the Revolution and committed suicide.

66 *Blok* (1880–1921): Most outstanding poet of the Symbolist school. He died, disillusioned with the Revolution.

67 *Mayakovsky* (1893–1930): A poet of the Futurist school. He became a great propagandist of the Revolution. Personal disasters and disillusionment with the Communists brought him to suicide. After his death he was taken up by Stalin and became a kind of official poet of the Revolution.

86 *Lermontov* (1814–41): A great Russian romantic poet and writer. The lines are taken from a poem written in 1836, when he was 22, entitled "The Wanderer's Prayer".

88 From a poem by Anna Akhmatova, written in 1922.

93 *Bubennov, Perventsev and Orest Maltsev*: minor Soviet novelists, who concentrated on putting across a particular theme in harmony with the Party line at the expense of any pretension to style.

95 *Meerovich*: journalist and critic.
Mikhoels (1890–1948): Outstanding Jewish actor and director. He became artistic director of the State Yiddish Theatre in 1929. The theatre was closed in 1948 during the campaign against "Cosmopolitanism" and for socialist Realism and Mikhoels perished a few months later.

110 *S.R.'s*: Socialist Revolutionaries. A political party founded in 1902 with a radical programme of reform. One of its tactics was assassination of leading govern-

ment personalities. The party was suppressed in 1922.

The Whites: the name given to the anti-Bolshevik forces during the civil war.

Denikin: In March 1918 he became commander of the anti-Bolshevik forces in Southern Russia. By November 1919 he had been completely defeated by the Bolsheviks. He died in exile in America.

119 *Herzen* (1812–70): Russian thinker and publicist. From 1847 he lived in exile and founded the journal '*Kolokol*' (Bell). Politically, he was a liberal socialist and opposed the idea that any abstract principle justified the sacrifice of individuals. Lydia Chukovskaya has herself written about Herzen.